POSSESSED BY THE DEVIL

NICOLA ROSE

Copyright © 2019 Nicola Rose
All Rights Reserved

Second Edition

No part of this publication may be reproduced or transmitted by any means, electronic, mechanical, photocopying or otherwise, without the prior written permission of the publisher.

This is a work of fiction. Whilst the towns/cities may be real, all other names, characters, businesses, and incidents are either the products of the author's imagination or are used fictitiously. The author acknowledges the trademarked status and trademark owners of various products referenced in this work of fiction, which have been used without permission. The publication/use of these trademarks is not authorized, associated with, or sponsored by the trademark owners.

Any similarity between the characters and situations within its pages and places or persons, living or dead, is unintentional and coincidental.

Visit the author's website
www.nicolarose-author.com

Cover Design: Ryn Katryn Book Art
Editing: J Culver
Proofreading: Lawrence Editing

For all the villain and anti-hero lovers...

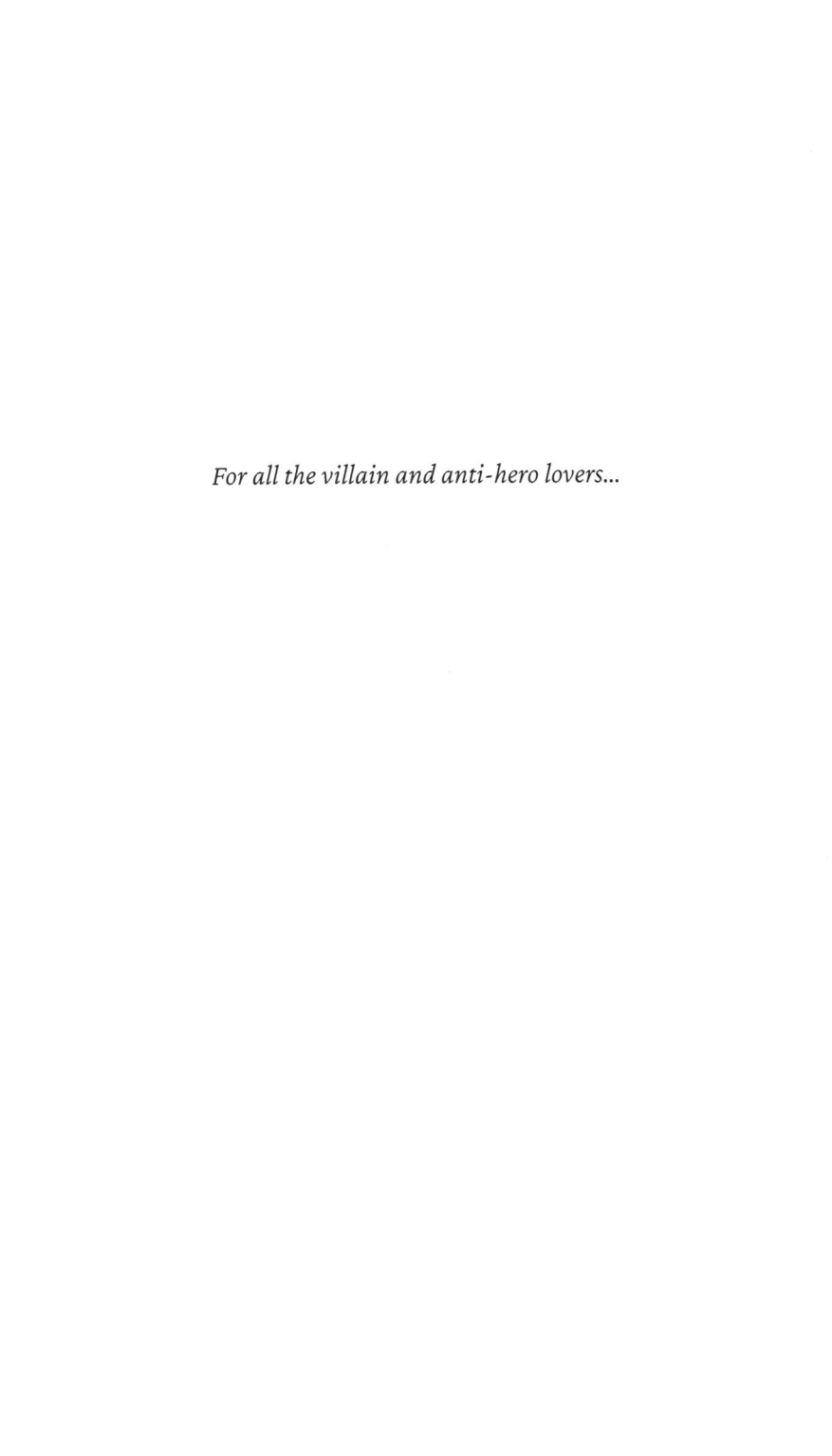

"We are each our own devil, and we make this world our hell."
Oscar Wilde

AUTHOR'S NOTE

This is a villain romance.
Lucifer is the *King of Hell*.
Don't be fooled by the pretty face. He's a monster wrapped up in a delicious package. He doesn't always play nice. And at times, you'll likely hate him for the things he does.
So buckle up for a quick, dark, steamy, and bloody ride!

If you are concerned about potential triggers, you can view a full content warning list on my website

www.nicolarose-author.com/content-warnings/

(Beware of minor spoilers for some books)

CHAPTER ONE

THERE'S A CERTAIN SMELL WHEN YOU SEND A DEMON BACK TO Hell.

It never leaves you. Once you've encountered that stink for the first time, it's always there in the back of your nose, in your subconscious—metallic, burnt wood, smoky, *nasty*.

But the more you kill, the more you get used to it.

I find that I almost like it these days. As soon as it hits my senses, I'm awake, on fire, *alive*.

This particular demon—my latest victim—thrashes inside a salt circle, head swinging violently from side to side, body shuddering. He'll smell rank when he dies, but he won't *look* it. They never do. Demons always pick the finest human hosts they can. Usually opting for tall, dark, and handsome. Standing before me is a suited businessman, impeccably dressed, chiseled jaw, good height and build.

With my feet kicked up onto the table, I lean back in

my chair, toying with the seraph blade in my hands. I've become attached to this blade. There have been plenty of others in the past, but this one feels special. I run my fingers over the intricate carvings on the handle and I swear the blade hums to me. Purring, softly vibrating, calling out for blood.

"You'll pay for this, bitch!" the demon yells, bloodied spit spraying from his mouth and over my boots.

Patiently, I rise to face him. "Very original. I've never heard that before."

These low-level demons can be so disappointing. Such an anticlimax.

I've been hunting this dick-weasel for weeks. Following him, tracking the innocent souls he's claimed, digging and digging until I finally found his name and was able to summon him here with a demon trap. There are plenty of other ways to summon or kill a demon, of course, but this is my favorite.

This way, you can take your sweet time. Go slowly. *Indulge.* Savor every moment.

He's surrounded by salt, trapped by symbols and spells—this jerk isn't going anywhere. Not until the moment I choose to send him back to Hell. Tingles erupt along my spine at the thought.

Suddenly he falls still, head slumped. Then his chin slowly lifts, and he spits in my face. I hadn't realized I'd drawn so close, studying those pitch-black eyes, falling into their chaos. I wonder what it must be like. The peace of having no soul, no guilt, no emotion whatsoever.

I drag my knife slowly down his cheek, not even

bothering to wipe away his spit. He cries out in agony, but I'm transfixed by the trickle of dark blood that ebbs toward his chin, tempted to have a little taste...

Boom!

An almighty crash thunders from outside the warehouse.

The demon grins.

"Oh, you naughty boy! Did you bring friends?" I smile back. Maybe this evening won't be such a disappointment after all. Drawing a second blade from its sheath on my leg, I sprint toward the sound of the commotion, hurl myself through a door, and burst out into the parking lot. Another explosion rocks the ground and I duck behind my truck amidst a downpour of rubble.

"Motherfucker!" I grumble, noticing a massive dent in the hood from flying debris. Fire blazes only feet away.

"Hey, Angel." A woman appears, crouching beside me. "Sorry about that." She nods to my ride.

"Brooke?" I peer at her through the dark. "What are you doing here?"

A bullet whizzes past my ear.

There looks to be a dozen hunters in the vicinity, all battling demons. Shoving my knives away, I draw a gun and begin shooting. A bullet won't kill a demon, but an enchanted one slows them down.

"We got a tip-off about demon activity in the building." Brooke shrugs, readying herself to dash across the lot, closer to the action.

"Wait." I grab her shoulder. "A tip-off from who?"

"I dunno. Why?"

"Shit! That piece of degenerate scum." Dodging bullets and flames, I speed back into the building, already knowing what I'm going to find.

A big, fat nothing.

The salt circle is broken. The symbols I'd carefully painted with my own blood have been smudged. And my demon is gone.

"Goddammit!" I kick over the chair I'd been sitting on earlier. Where I'd put my feet up and taunted him with my nonchalance. *Sloppy.*

'Don't mess around, Angel. You must be able to protect yourself. Kill and run. Never stay still.' My dad's voice slices through the ringing in my ears.

How the hell had he managed to call for human backup? No demon could have got inside my circle to destroy my spells. My victim had to have had human help. All that shit going down outside was just a distraction while he escaped.

And here I was thinking he was just a bottom-dwelling turd.

"Game on, douche-nozzle. You just landed yourself on my priority shit list," I yell into the heavy air inside the warehouse.

Gunshots crack outside. My target might be gone, but they're still fighting out there. He must have been high up to summon others to his side. A normal grunt would get zero assistance from his fellow demons. They only care about themselves; they don't form bonds or connections or allegiances. Self-serving, they deal in lies, death, and dodgy deals.

How had I missed this?

You know exactly how... the dark voice inside me taunts. Not my dad's voice, ringing through me in waves of memory, but something else entirely. It's always worse at this time of year, putting me off my game, unsettling me.

Cursing, I slump back into the chair, uninspired to join the fight outside. I hate working with other hunters, even on a good day. If I were here alone, I'd be out there destroying the enemy and loving every second. But right now, I feel a little stupid and a *lot* pissed that there's a bunch of other hunters on my turf.

I mean, Brooke's sweet, I guess. Probably the closest I've ever had to a friend. She always tries to engage with me when our paths cross. But the others? Meh. I have no interest.

Boom!

Another explosion. More shouting.

It shouldn't be taking this long for them to put down a few demons. I'm confident I could have dealt with it all alone by now. Inhaling a deep breath—annoyingly devoid of the expected *exorcised-demon* smell—I trudge back outside.

"You do know this is my warehouse? I use it all the time for summoning when I'm in the city." I position myself next to Brooke, shooting a demon-bitch between the eyes as she charges us.

With all these hunters here, it's going to be excruciating after the fight. I'll have to go around nodding and smiling and enduring all the high fives and back patting. I have the strongest temptation to dig my heels in and claim dibs, send them all packing.

But sometimes you must pick those battles. They're harder to navigate than the actual flesh and blood brawls. And they aren't always worth fighting.

'Sometimes you have to play nice and share,' Dad would say. But he wasn't talking about sharing my toys like a normal parent. No, he was talking about sharing my *kills*. I guess I've always been a selfish bitch when it comes to death.

I'm so busy obsessing over this hatred of working with others that I don't notice the big-ass demon who's crept up behind me until his hands are around my throat.

Dropping my gun, I grab a knife from my hip and try to stab him, but he switches in a lightning flash to holding me by my neck with just one hand. His other hand grabs the knife, barely flinching as it slices his palm. He yanks it from my grip, tossing it across the lot.

"Hey, that's my best blade!" I gasp.

"Luckily, you won't be needing it anymore." He smirks in that irritating cocky way all demons do.

Frantically trying to retrieve one of the many other weapons stashed on my body, I keep muttering obscenities in the hope he won't pay attention to my desperate fumbling.

It's no good.

I dropped the gun in favor of my knife, and now I can't reach the blades in my boots.

And I can't fucking *breathe*.

Come on, Angel, you've been in far worse predicaments than this before, the shadowy voice in my head helpfully points out. Unlike the memories of my dad's voice, this is real and present—my own self-torment, conscience, whatever you want to call it. But it never sounds like me. I always use a male voice when I'm talking to myself. Serious daddy issues, I suppose.

Crossed with split personality, maybe?

The world dims. I can't see much.

My lungs *burn...*

His lips open in a silent scream, black smoke erupting from his throat, shooting up into the sky in an angry, swirling stream, on and on and on...

Eventually, it stops. His mouth falls shut. He blinks, eyes going from all black to the normal blue irises of a human. There's a second, so very brief, when I always think they're alive... but the human host dies the instant they're claimed. No coming back. So no, I don't feel guilty about the way I torture demons, make them bleed. It's just a demon, no human present.

He slumps to the ground, the momentum pulling me with him. The grip on my throat loosens. I disentangle myself, stand up, and dust down, choking on the stink as I drag much-needed breath back into my lungs.

Brooke stands there, wiping off the angel blade she stuck between his shoulders against her pants.

"I could've handled that. I was just toying with him."

I stoop to retrieve my own precious blade.

The parking lot has fallen silent. All demons vanquished. All hunters paused for breath. I subconsciously rub at my neck, already feeling the pain from bruising.

"You're welcome!" Brooke grins, all white teeth and warmth, grabbing me for a hug. It doesn't matter how much of a bitch I am; she never gets pissed with me. "And you're right, I'm sure you *could* have handled it, but the point is, you didn't need to. Learn to accept help, Angel. It won't kill you."

Releasing me from the hideous show of affection, Brooke saunters away to join her friends. Predictably, they fall into an easy routine of chatter and praise about the fight, showing off new injuries, gathering weapons back, finishing off any demons who were only down and not out.

I stand there awkwardly for a moment, then try to sneak away—

"Hey, Angel!" one of the guys calls out.

No, please no. I die a little more on the inside. *Don't ask, please don't ask...*

"You coming to The Salty Haven?"

My stomach sinks through my boots.

"Hunter rules," Brooke calls out in her teasing tone. *Teasing, but true.* "Hunters who live to see another day after working together *must* drink together. Don't go breaking that code and cursing us all!"

May the Devil have mercy on me because this is going to be hell.

CHAPTER TWO

Stupid *Hunter Code*.

What a crock of horseshit.

I never play by the rules. I work alone. They know this. And yet, Brooke gives me that smile, and I don't feel like I can say no.

Such a pussy when it comes to humans. You can gut a demon in seconds without blinking, but you can't say no to a human request of friendship?

"Come on, give me a smile." Brooke nudges my shoulder as I exit my beat-up truck and we walk slowly toward her bar. "You never play with us. We finally got to share a fight with you. Give these guys something back. You're like a celebrity to them, you know?"

I scoff, rolling my eyes.

My palms feel clammy.

The Salty Haven. Only hunters are allowed through the doors ahead. Those big blue doors that suddenly seem like the most imposing things I've ever seen in my life—

"*Relax.*" Brooke pulls me to a stop and forces me to face her. "They're just people, Angel. People who think you're the baddest, most kick-ass hunter in the whole stinkin' world. Smile, talk shit with them for an hour, then you can leave."

Nodding once, I try to smile, but my face refuses to cooperate.

With a resigned sigh, Brooke pushes through the door and disappears. It's all right for her. She manages this place and she loves it. It's her home.

I take a deep breath. Then another and another.

Wiping my palms on my cargo pants, I take another step. Something dark flashes past the corner of my eye. Swinging around, I scan the area, hand poised over my gun.

There's a rustle in the bushes, but that's all. Peering into the night, I try to work out what it was. It flashes by again, this time from the left, just out of my main vision, but I detect the motion, see the dark shadow as it zips past.

I will not fear the shadows. I embrace the shadows.

I spin in a circle, drawing my weapon.

"Who's there?" I shout, which is a surprisingly effective tactic. Demons are so vain they can't resist stepping out and revealing themselves.

Another trace of something dark, right on the edge of my vision. No matter how fast I spin around, I can't get a good look at it. There one second, gone the next.

I can't see the shadowy shape lurking anywhere, but I can feel its presence *everywhere.*

All around. Watching. Waiting. Silently assessing me.

I will not fear the shadows...

I repeat the mantra to myself. One of these days, it might actually sink in, and my body might agree. For now, my heart beats so hard I think it's going to snap a rib.

"Seriously, how long does it take for you to talk yourself into this? Get your butt in here, sister!" Brooke reappears, holding the door.

Holstering my gun, I move away from my demon stalker, into the midst of something far scarier.

There's a whole chain of Salty Havens across the country. You can find one in almost every city. Magically warded so that *normal* humans barely notice them and never feel the urge to step inside.

Dad used to drag me to every Haven he could find as we traveled around in our nomadic way. I hated it. He never seemed happy either, but we still went. All the hunters would talk about why and how they became hunters. It was like a rite of passage when you entered a new bar—you told them your story. I listened to so many of theirs, which were likely embellished with every retelling to make them more dramatic.

But no matter how many times I heard Dad's story, it never changed. There was never any glory, any passion, any emotion. It was short and simple. *'I became a hunter because what else could I do once I found demons existed?'*

Well. 'Run and hide like most' was the obvious reply.

He told his story like it made perfect sense, but something was missing, and I never could work out what it was. But I do know the extent of his obsession could not have come from such a simple story. To all those hunters in the bars, it was a job. They went home to their families, they tried to forget what they'd seen, and they *lived*.

Not us. There was never anything other than hunting. I didn't exactly have a conventional childhood. We bounced from town to town. Dad had a load of money from inheritance—which has ended up in my pockets—but he'd also take on labor work here and there. At first, when I was young, he would get me into different schools for a month or so. By the time I was ten, I was done with that charade, and so was he.

He'd trained me to fight from the day I could walk.

And here I am, back in a Haven after so many blissful years away from them, only this time I don't have my father for backup.

You'd think that having a *hunters only* bar, going by the same name in every city, would make them a target for all things supernatural to attack. But these places are heavily warded and, obviously, crammed to the rafters with hunters just itching for a demon to attack.

For this reason, they usually stay away.

Which is why I feel especially uneasy about the shadowy *thing* that was teasing me outside.

The anxiety is soon forgotten, replaced with another,

as a group of hunters immediately swarm me, getting too close, all up in my personal space with an avalanche of questions and anecdotes and never-ending camaraderie.

"So, the name Angel?" someone says.

Ugh. Here we go. For the millionth time.

Thanks, Dad. I'm sure you thought it was a real funny idea to call your kid Angel, knowing full well you were going to raise her as a hunter.

In truth, though, it was more than just a joke. Yeah, he claimed it was for shits and giggles, but I think he really believed it might give me some extra sway with the big G himself. Like God would surely offer his precious daughter some extra special protection, a little boost here and there, since she'd be out there doing his dirty work, clearing up the mess.

Dad should have known better. Angels are barely any better than demons. *Pretentious assholes.*

"Yeah. I'm a real angel, so don't mess with me," I mutter. They laugh at my joke like I'm the shit.

The room's starting to spin.

I haven't been this tense since the day a demon managed to trap me with my own spells, dangling me upside-down by chains around my ankles, slowly raking his claws over my naked body—

"No fucking way!" A skinny dude wearing full tactical combat gear is standing so close that I can feel his beer breath on my face. "You were the hunter who managed to break through reverse-warded chains and defeat *Asmodeus*?"

Shit! Did I reveal that thought out loud? *This is why I don't do people-ing.*

Deep laughter whispers past my ear, but it's not coming from any of the guys who are crowding me, open-mouthed, waiting for a response. It felt more like it was inside my head. A low, rumbling chuckle.

I excuse myself with a nod and a, "*Yep, that was me,*" then head to the restroom. The door slams behind me as I charge inside, grabbing the basin and leaning my forehead into the mirror above it.

I need to get a grip. I'm always edgy around this time of year, but this is ridiculous. Socializing with a bunch of decent, like-minded people should *not* cause this panic.

I splash cold water over my face.

'Sssssssssssssssssssss.' A spine-tingling whisper whooshes right into my ears. I can almost feel the chill of cool breath on the back of my neck.

A dark shape passes on the very edge of my vision as if passing through the stalls; it moves across and *through* them. Nothing in the mirror looks different, but I felt it. I saw it.

The shadows inside the stalls are deep, calling me, sucking me in—

The door slams open. I practically leap out of my own skin, reflexively grabbing my knife.

A woman cautiously walks past me, eyeing the knife and holding her hands up. "Sorry to startle you." Her brows pinch in confusion before she shakes her head and enters a stall, staring at me like I'm crazy.

I embrace the shadows. I know exactly what goes bump in the night and I hunt it down.

I turn back to the mirror. I guess I do look a little wide-eyed. A touch frayed around the edges.

The woman does her business, washes up, and leaves. I'm still staring at myself. I don't recognize the woman staring back. I don't know who I am. There's a disconnect between what I feel on the inside and what I project to the world.

But there's only so much my hard-ass exterior can do to distract from the lost girl, dead on the inside, missing her dad, and way too conscious of the shadows all around.

My heart is still skyrocketing. It launched into space ages ago and shows no sign of returning.

Something's coming. Waiting for me.

It's nothing new. I should be used to it by now, but somehow it seems to get harder each year instead of easier. I used to think it was just me, back in the early days when I was a kid. In the run-up to every birthday, I'd start getting this ominous feeling, start seeing and hearing things.

But I quickly noted that the difference in my dad's behavior mirrored my own around that date. In fact, by the end, it was driving him positively mad.

"It's the same every year. Nothing happens, Angel. Get over it. Put the jitters aside," I talk to my reflection.

Another door creaks open, making me gasp. Brooke vacates a stall and washes her hands. Had she been in there all along? Or had I not even noticed her come in?

"You losing your shit, Angel? Talking to yourself is the first sign, you know." She gives me a sad smile in the mirror. She's not even joking.

"I lost my shit long ago. Maybe around that time I gutted a demon and did a rain dance in his blood? Or there was that time when I was eight years old and Dad showed me how to make their eyes pop out with the right spells."

Brooke laughs awkwardly as I retie my hair into a tight ponytail. No one gets my sense of humor, not even her. It might be true, but it's still funny. *Right?*

CHAPTER
THREE

I wake up with the most excruciating pain stabbing through my skull. My mouth feels like the dusty insides of a vacuum cleaner. *Everything* hurts.

My eyes open slowly, dreading what I'll see, expecting to find myself holed up in some demon's filthy hovel. Bracing myself for the torture that's to come...

All I see is blinding light streaming through a gap in the drapes. A desk littered with books and files and coffee cups. My boots discarded with my clothes in a chaotic mess from the doorway to my bed.

Nope. I'm not hostage to the scourge of Hell. I just have a hangover.

Ugh, and this is why I don't drink.

No people-ing and no drinking. Top rules.

I empty out the bedside cabinet, looking for the painkillers I stashed when I came back to this city a week ago. Brief snippets of memory bombard me. Events from the previous night... of me deciding to quit being such a baby and let loose, party with these people.

My people! Embrace them, laugh with them, down fifteen shots of some blue shit with them!

My phone buzzes. After a little swaying on my feet, I manage to find it in my cargo pants' pocket. I pull them on while I'm up, fearing I may never stand again once I sit back on the hotel bed.

The screen informs me I have a message from *'Brooke aka my best friend and hunter extraordinaire'*.

What the fuck! I swapped numbers with her?

I consider deleting the message without reading it, but my finger presses the open button.

Hey, Angel. Last night was amazing. Who knew you could deep throat a beer bottle like that? Certainly not the twenty guys in the Salty Haven! Or the twenty thousand people who've watched the TikTok!

I groan, flopping onto my back.

Kidding! I'm kidding! Another message comes through. *There was no video. You're safe. Tell me you're coming back tonight for your birthday? You promised me, Angel. And a Hunter never breaks their word.*

I told her my *birthday*?! I've crossed over so many of my own boundaries in one night. Closing my eyes, I reassure myself that it's fine. I'm going to leave this city. Tomorrow.

Just as soon as I'm physically able to stand without the room wobbling and I've done what I came here for.

Maybe you need company. Maybe it's good for you? Maybe it's time to find solace in the arms of

someone other than yourself and your cold, dead heart?

Stupid voice of reason. Even more irritating than the Hunter's Code. Shutting it down, I breathe deep and focus on getting back to sleep.

HE WATCHES ME FROM THE SHADOWS.

No, not from them... he is the shadows.

They wisp and coil behind him, alive and ominous. As he steps forward, the darkness moves with him, clinging to his skin like a malicious entity all of its own.

My gaze lifts and I know every inch of that painfully pretty face. Far too beautiful for a monster.

I've been addicted to staring at him since I was eighteen years old.

I suck in a breath at the way his eyes shift from all black to red. At how magnificent they are. I should feel terrified, I should whimper and cower, but they're so intoxicating. I don't see a beast. I see the only man who can truly make me tremble with pleasure.

He's naked. All hard muscle and knee-weakening contours. There's blood splattered across his chest... as if he's sliced someone's throat and it sprayed over him. It draws my attention, luring me in like the junkie I am.

He doesn't need to issue the command. I know it's coming, so I rush to him, stooping down to lick the crimson staining his beautiful skin. I start at his nipple, my tongue swirling circles around it before sucking.

He fists my hair, pushing me down. Resisting his pressure, I move slowly, enjoying the metallic taste as I clean up his abs. Taking the time to cleanse every ridge, every hard plane of solid muscle.

Growling, he shoves me to my knees, tired of my patience in getting to his cock.

Licking my lips, I look up into those glowing red eyes, batting my lashes, a smirk on my face—

He shoves himself into my mouth, hitting the back of my throat. I gag, but he won't let up. He pumps into me, holding me tightly by my hair.

He's going to treat me rough tonight. Just like most nights, except those rare few that leave me confused. But tonight, there will be spankings and chains and devices... pain.

The blissful release that only his pain can bring me. Exquisite, freeing, liberating...

"Not today, my Angel," he says in that deep, rumbling voice that melts my insides. "From today, you're going to have to work a little harder to be granted that release."

My eyes snap open.

I land back into reality with a groan. My head still hurts, my mind instantly whirs to life with the dread of what today is, and there's this unbearable ache in my core, the need to finish what started in the dream, arousal running rampant through my veins.

The dreams started when I was eighteen. Always so deliciously dark and devious.

I've slept with a few men to satisfy brief moments of need, but I've never done anything like what I do in my dreams. Real life is usually pretty vanilla. Sometimes they'll rough me up a little, grab my hair, throw me around… it's never enough, and I can't be bothered to educate them. There's no point. I don't stick around for any longer than one night.

I'm so damned horny. I could finish myself off, deal with the lingering frustration of not getting the sleepy climax I'm accustomed to, but my eyes snag to a folder on the desk and I haul ass out of bed.

Today is a special day.

Grabbing the file that sits atop a stack, I rifle through the papers inside, spreading them over the desk and knocking an empty cup to the floor. Cursing, I reach down to retrieve it—

Whump!

Something else hits the floor in the en suite, making me jump and crack my head on the desk.

For fuck's sake! Hunters don't get jittery. It's just like any other day.

I left the window open in there. Something has just fallen in the breeze. That's all.

Breathe. One, two. In, out.

I embrace the shadows.

Still, I grab my gun as I cautiously approach the bathroom and flick the light. It's almost dark. I slept all damned day.

The shampoo rocks gently on the floor where it fell. I slam the window closed, despite there being no breeze. After putting the bottle back, I turn to leave—

A pair of glowing eyes assess me from behind the frosted shower screen.

"You know, it's rude to take a shower in someone else's room unless you're invited!" I yank the screen, ready to shoot.

Of course, it's empty.

The same creepy shit every birthday.

I peer back through to my room, warily eyeing the shadow cast by the closet. Yes, I'm a hunter who's uneasy about shadows. Okay, there. I said it.

Give me a bloodthirsty demon and I'm fine, but put me somewhere with deep shadows in the corners and I start sweating. It's not that I'm afraid of what's hiding in them. I already know, and monsters don't scare me.

It's the shadows *themselves*, which I know is ridiculous. But this stupid, irrational anxiety has been with me my whole life and I can't shift it.

Huffing in frustration, I return to my file. A rugged, handsome face stares at me from a grainy photograph.

Asmodeus.

I always save myself a special case for my birthday. Partly because, hello, birthday! I don't have any family or friends to shower me with gifts, so I give myself something. But mostly it's because I'm always such a ball of crazy nervous energy on my birthday that I need to keep busy. It takes a real challenge, not the mundane day-to-day shit.

So, if a demon catches my attention during the year and I know he's going to be a goodun', then I wait. I file him away until my big day. Indulge myself in a treat, my gift to me. A reward for how hard I work.

Asmodeus caught my attention years ago, in an epic way. Neither of us came out of it the same. But ultimately, I won, sending him back to Hell. And now he's here again, walking the earth without a care in the world.

We have unfinished business. After what he did to me, I was too hasty, killing him when the brief window of opportunity appeared. I ended him in a heartbeat, driving my seraph blade right between his eyes.

That loss still haunts me. He's a seriously high-level demon, a Prince of Hell, no less. I wanted to make him suffer. I wanted *time* to enjoy it, draw it out, play with him.

And that's why I'm back in this city, where I can use my favorite, extra powerfully warded warehouse. Don't talk to me about the demon and hunter invasion the other night. Too late to worry about that now. I just have to hope my wards are still strong.

This time, I'm going to get the *fun* out of him. Asmodeus owes me.

CHAPTER
FOUR

I'VE PACKED UP ALL MY SHIT. LITERALLY, *ALL* MY SHIT.

Not just the gear I need for hunting a demon *prince*, but everything I own. Once this is done, I'm leaving. Brooke and her band of merry hunters are getting way too familiar. I've had three more text messages in the space of five minutes about the party they're throwing me at the Salty Haven. One message from Brooke, and I have no idea who owns the other two random numbers. Looks like I had a great time dishing out my contact details while partying with them.

I don't know what came over me.

Well, yes, I do. Like I said, I always go nuts on my birthday.

Anything to avoid thinking about Dad, about how I found him on my seventeenth birthday, brains blown out. Or about all the creepy shit that haunts me on the day itself and the week preceding it.

Nope.

Don't think, don't feel. Move forward.

I don't look back as my feet hit the sidewalk outside the hotel. Walking round to retrieve my truck, I focus on the task ahead, muttering as I run through the plan. I make sure I have every detail down, every Plan A and B and C. These demons like to test us and throw unexpected shit our way.

Summoning Asmodeus into my demon trap will take huge skill, especially since I've tried and failed once before. But I've spent years studying where I went wrong, and I'm certain I've got it right this time.

Skidding into the warehouse parking lot, I grab my shit from the trunk and pause outside the door. There are still some suspicious patches on the gravel, but all the bodies are gone, most of the blood cleaned away. Who did this? It's my turf. I should have carried out the cleanup operation. I mean, I would have, but there was the bar, and the drinking, and then the sleeping...

Another favor I'm going to have to thank Brooke for. She fixed up this war zone while I slumbered in my hotel, dreaming about a red-eyed monster with the pleasure skills of a debauched sex god.

Speak of the Devil. My voice of inner torment surfaces, along with the shadowy presence whooshing around the edge of my vision. **Happy Birthday.**

Thunder explodes directly overhead, shattering a window. Glass sprays into my face, peppering me with tiny pricks of pain. I wipe my cheek, smearing blood along the back of my hand. *What the...?*

There's not a storm cloud in sight. No rain, no wind; a clear blue sky!

I should leave.

I know this.

'If in doubt, run. Don't stay still. Don't let him trap you...'

"Who, Dad?" I yell into the summer sky. "Don't let *who* trap me? You have no right running through my head with your bullshit words of wisdom. You left me!" My knees threaten to buckle.

I can't take another birthday like this. I can't handle the shadows and the voices and the *waiting*.

Waiting for the death that never comes.

The warehouse door swings open so violently that it splinters and hangs from the hinges, bouncing back from the wall. I gape, open-mouthed.

I will not let these birthday intimidation games put me off my kill.

I will not leave.

Angel. My name is called out from nowhere, from *everywhere*.

I will not run.

I will not succumb to the churning unease that's making my legs weak. It's just another birthday, just like all the others. Just another day in my own private horror show.

Wrong. This time it's different.

"Fuck you!" I scream, launching into action.

It takes only ten minutes to set up my trap. I already have a ton of spells marked out in this building. They only need refreshing. A little more of my blood, some salt, some tweaks, and I'm ready.

Thunder continues to crack overhead. The building literally vibrates with ominous energy. Ignoring it, I speak the required words.

One long rush of wind races through the room, blowing out my candles, so the only light is from the broken windows. Then there's silence.

So disturbingly quiet in the wake of the storm that my ears hum.

Asmodeus materializes in the center of my trap, fists clenched within the chains he's found himself in. I step back involuntarily from his gaze. It's all menace and pure, unbridled carnage, just waiting to rain down on my ass.

"Not today, my prince," I speak, forcing myself to step forward again. "Pack away those thoughts you're having, because this time the only one being strung upside down and slowly picked apart will be you."

He laughs.

For a long time.

I wait for him to finish, raising my eyebrows. He can't seriously think he's getting out this time?

"Angel," he whispers, letting the L at the end linger on his tongue. "There's *nothing* but submission in your future. Enjoy this while you can."

His smug smile has me lashing out, punching him in the face. His head whips to the side, blood spraying from his nose. He just laughs more.

"*Efflo*," I say, staring hard into his charcoal eyes.

His smile drops. His eyes widen. His breathing becomes shallow and labored. The panic slowly creeps through him, building in intensity, fueling my darkest desires. I'll never tire of this thrill.

I watch as his eyes roll in his head, and he gasps like a fish out of water. I'm pretty sure demons technically don't need to breathe. But that's the beauty of this spell... it makes them think they do. All the more entertaining as they suddenly find it harder and harder, suffocating on their own black demon smoke as it clogs their throats.

His body twitches. He groans and gasps before going limp. *Shit!* He could actually clock out... too soon! "*Respiro!*" I hastily shout.

To my relief, he takes a huge drag of air and his eyes snap back to alert.

"Very good. What else do you have? Ticktock." He smiles.

Eyeing him dubiously, I step behind him, where he can't keep those malicious eyes on me.

I reach out, touching my fingertips between his shoulder blades. He flinches, trying to turn round, but the hexed chains hold him tight. Dipping a finger into the bowl beside me, filled with a mixture of herbs and animal blood, I paint a reverse cross on his back. "*Demeto pellis,*" I urge.

"No!" he yells.

I'm fascinated by the sight that appears before me. I've never done this one before. I wasn't certain it would work. But his skin starts to blister around the painted cross, and little wisps of black demon smoke snake their way out of him, drifting up to the rafters. His demon essence leaving the host. This could be the slowest exorcism I've ever performed. Enthralled, I grab a chair and sit down to watch. He's trembling with fear or rage or maybe just the exertion of trying to hold himself inside the body as he slowly leaks out.

It keeps me entertained for a while, but before long, I need to see his eyes. I want him staring at me as he dies. Repositioning myself with a front-row view, I search his face for signs of his pain.

Yes, I know, I'm *sick*. I blame Dad. I mean, when you start helping your father to kill monsters as soon as you can walk, it becomes an obsession. It's addictive. But the more you do it, the less satisfying it becomes, and that just makes you want more. Constantly seeking new and improved ways to find the thrill, going bigger and grander and bloodier.

Asmodeus is doing an impressive job of locking down his pain. Grinding his teeth, focusing on the floor by my feet. Every muscle in his body tight and strained. Veins stick out all along his arms, up his neck, across his temples.

"Look at me," I shout.

He does so without hesitation, and a spike of pure fear rushes through me.

His demon spirit is draining away. He should be looking more worried by this point, but he's suddenly the perfect mask of calm. His arms tense and the chains around his wrists seem to sizzle with the strain of holding him. The magical symbols on the chains glow brighter, and then flicker, stuttering.

I reach for my seraph blade.

This doesn't feel right.

"*Citius*," I growl. Maybe time to speed this up after all. I *am* playing with a prince here, and maybe I've been too casual. The black smoke erupts from his back in a quickening stream.

Still, he grinds his jaw, eyes tracking me as I move around the room, painting a few extra protection and holding symbols onto the walls.

A black shape streaks in my peripheral. Once, twice... three times. I can't catch sight of it for long enough.

Asmodeus chuckles. Quiet and genuine. Not like the usual loud and cocky laughter these demons like to exude. This is calm and assured.

One of the chains snaps on his left wrist.

"Crap!" Gripping my blade hard, I rush to slice his throat.

A mere second before the metal meets his skin, his head falls back, mouth open in a gaping yawn, and the rest of his demon essence explodes from his throat in a savage plume of black smoke. It's so brutal that his jaw splits apart, hanging down, dangling in some obscene way.

It seems to go on forever as I slowly sheath my blade, confused as fuck.

Once every bit of demon is exorcised, his body slumps against the chains. *Dead*.

The room is once again deathly silent in the wake of

the violent exorcism. I've never seen a demon spirit leave a body like that, so fast and frantic, wild and savage.

Beautiful.

All I can hear is my own heavy breathing and the thudding of my heart in my ears.

But I know I'm not alone.

Something is behind me.

Silent. Predatory. *Waiting.*

I feel its presence like a terrifying cloak around my shoulders. It's heavy, malevolent, and I'm too unnerved to turn around.

But it's not moving.

It's *still* waiting.

My fingers creep slowly to my gun. Then I change my mind and reach for the blade again. Whatever this thing is, it's not human, and I don't think a bullet is going to hurt it. Even the shadows on the far side of the room are expanding, reaching out for me.

They're just shadows...

The door is too far away. I could try to bolt, but it's risky.

No.

Turn and face it.

I don't want to!

It's going to be like some demon hellhound, all snarling fangs and mangy body, twisted and deformed and hideous. Nothing else could *feel* like this. Could fill the room with such heavy menace that it chokes the air. I've seen some nasty creatures before, but I don't think I'm ready to face this one.

Why is it still waiting? Why hasn't it attacked?

We're at a stalemate, neither wanting to force the encounter. Both waiting for the other to make the first move.

The thunder resumes its dramatic melody overhead. *It's a summer day out there!*

I thought Asmodeus had caused the sound earlier, but had this creature been hiding here all along? Stalking me?

I feel its breath down the back of my neck. It's so close, all around me—in front, behind, overhead, *everywhere*! I'm just waiting for its hideous claws to rake down my back and yank my spine from my body, but I can't move to defend myself.

I'm frozen.

I can't let this go on.

Turn around. Turn around. Turn around.

Turn around.

The command in my head switches to that deep, drawling tone. The male voice that matches the one in my dreams.

"Fuck it!" I yell. "Come on then, you fetid pit-dwelling fucking maggot!"

Spinning around, drawing my blade in a flash, I brandish it before me, ready to slice and hack and defend myself from the onslaught—

A man leans against the far wall.

One hand in his pocket, wearing only faded jeans and boots. One leg cocked, his boot against the bricks behind him. Striking some sort of model pose with his muscled chest, spiky hair and youthful, handsome face.

His damned *gorgeous* face.

That face.

The jaw, the lips...

I've bitten them before. I've stared at that face so hard it nearly made my eyes bleed with its beauty.

Gasping, I stumble backward, crashing into the chair. Righting myself, I move behind it, trying to put something, *anything*, between us.

"You're... you're..." I try.

He offers a bemused smile, eyebrows cocked.

"I'm...? What?"

That *voice*! The masculinity and authority, the drawl that makes me want to surrender everything I am!

Pushing from the wall, he stalks forward, emanating such menace, nothing but smooth, controlled power. Stuffing both hands in his pockets, he saunters closer, and the shadows behind him pull together, drawing into a shape, into... wings. Shadowy, smoky wings that are there, but aren't there. Not solid, but dragging energy from the room, coiling and warping, dark and sinister.

His black eyes shine in a way that demon eyes shouldn't. They're usually just orbs of matte darkness, dead and lifeless, but his *sparkle*.

Sometimes they turn red.

I know this.

How do I know this?

"My dreams," I cry out. "It's you."

He nods thoughtfully. And I can feel the patronizing

comment coming before it arrives; how I should have realized sooner, given that I have those dreams almost every night. But he can't be real, he can't—

"The King of Hell." He smiles, tipping his head to the side, eyeing me up and down. "It's a pleasure to finally meet you."

"The King of Hell," I repeat in a flat tone.

He smiles. Dazzling. Annoyingly breathtaking.

"*The* King of Hell," I state.

"The one and only."

And then I laugh.

So loud and insane, I almost pee my pants.

"You should probably take a seat?" He nods to the chair.

I stop laughing. Glare at him.

"Seriously, take the seat," he urges.

I stare him down.

"In three, two, one—"

My legs give out and I find myself on my knees, clutching for breath that won't come.

"If you're this stubborn about the simple command of taking a seat, I can't wait to see what comes next," he whispers in my ear as his hands go under my armpits and he hauls me into the chair as if I weigh nothing.

"*The* King of Hell." I should probably be trying to stab him, muttering spells, escaping... but all I can think about is the orgasms he's been giving me in my dreams.

Every. Damned. Night.

"I've spent my entire adult life dreaming about *Satan* fucking me?" I groan.

"I seriously hope not. If Satan has been on your mind instead of me, then we have a problem."

My face scrunches in confusion.

"Satan is an entirely different being. Not seen him for centuries."

I choke on something between a laugh, snort, and incredulous gasp. "So, what do I call you? The King of Hell seems a bit long. And egotistical."

He grins at this. "Most people call me Sir, my King, Master. Let's start there and see how you go."

This time, my choking laugh makes my eyes water.

He ignores me, eyes sliding to the crumpled heap on the floor. The body that housed Asmodeus.

Asmodeus. One of the strongest demons there is, who suddenly died way too quickly with me barely touching him.

"*You* killed Asmodeus! Isn't he a *Prince* of Hell? That's how you treat your princes?"

Keep him talking. Get your mind out of the gutter with his hot body and insanely competent cock, and start thinking about how to shred this douche and get out of this alive...

Kill the King of Hell.

Is there any greater hit to get on your résumé? I might even willingly go back to the Salty Haven with a story like this to tell.

He shrugs. "I treat them the same as anyone else. If they fuck with me or mine, they pay the price. Asmodeus has spent the last three years in the infernal dungeon in a state of perpetual torture because of what he did to you. I only let him out so that I could watch you hunt him down all over again. Give the big birthday showdown you're always searching for. Consider it my first gift to you, Angel."

I have an increasing urge to slap that smile right off his pretty face. "If it was truly a gift to me, then you'd have let *me* finish him off."

"Ah, yes. Unfortunately, you're not quite as strong as you think you are. Asmodeus would have overcome you once again, so I saved you, just like the first time."

"What?" I shriek, finding my feet and pressing the tip of my blade against his chest. "I stabbed him between the eyes with this seraph blade. He was *mine!*"

He calmly looks down at the weapon that's ready to pierce his heart and send him back to Hell. "You think an ordinary angel blade is enough to condemn a demon prince? Or the King? Oh, Angel, you still have so much to learn. I'll enjoy your education—"

"Eat shit!" I slam the blade into his stomach, buried to the hilt, and drag it upward.

At this point, per my experience, the demons begin writhing in pain as their blackened soul erupts from their body, cast back to the pit.

He simply smiles.

I grab another blade from my boot and swipe it across his throat.

The flesh splits apart, but instead of blood or smoke pouring out, the wound simply knits back together.

Springing back, I begin muttering every spell I can think of that might help.

He vanishes before my eyes. One second there, the next... gone.

There are flashes of darkness. Black shapes that start to form on the edge of my vision and then disappear, always too fast to focus on. Invisible fingers trailing up my spine. Whispering chuckles in my ears...

"Motherfucker! It was *you*? Every birthday? All the creepy heebie-jeebie shit?" I scream into the empty room.

And then he's solid again. Right before me. So close that his lips are almost touching mine.

Real. So very real... and warm... burning heat radiating—

"Enough time wasting." He takes my hand, and the world falls away.

CHAPTER
FIVE

You might think you know what Hell would be like, should it be real. Or at least have an idea of what to expect.

You don't.

I thought I knew what to expect. I've talked to hunters who've been here. Or rather, I've listened as they bragged. My own attempts at opening a hellgate have always failed. And now, being here, I can't believe I ever *wanted* to come.

I'm not prepared. I don't think anything could prepare for this. This feeling—so intense, so dark and ominous, pressing over you like a tangible weight. It bears down on your shoulders, making it hard to breathe.

It's like the gravity is *stronger*. Painfully oppressive.

And the noise? I feel like I can hear distant screaming, so far away it's almost not there. No matter which way I angle my head, I can't get a better grip on it, can't work out where it's coming from.

I don't need him to tell me this is Hell. It's so vastly different to home, it can't be anything else.

We stand atop a mountain, observing the expanse below. Sweeping plains of black rock, edged by ominous, craggy mountains. It's all rock. No plants or trees or water. Just these obsidian crags and boulders that are threaded with glowing orange veins.

I touch one, expecting it to burn. The delicate spirals threaded through the rock look like molten lava, and it *does* feel hot to the touch, but not scorching.

But by far, the most surprising thing is what's nestled amidst the outcrops—whole towns and cities. The buildings are too far away for me to determine what they're made of, but they're all as black as the rocks around them.

Demons live in houses? Cities?!

The sky glows red, and I have a feeling it never changes. Perpetual sunset, but there's no sun. Even so, the sweat beads on my brow and my clothes cling.

It's kind of beautiful. Stunning in its raw, intimidating darkness... much like the King of Hell who stands beside me, gazing upon his kingdom with a barely contained smirk.

I have so many questions, but I hold my tongue and ask the only one that really matters right now. "You're too pretty to be the Devil. You look like you're barely out of puberty."

Wait. *What?!* No, that wasn't what I meant to ask. That wasn't even a damned question.

And it isn't true. Sure, he has a young face, but the aura surrounding him commands subservience. He looks like he could break me in one blink of an eye.

Still, my statement has the desired effect. I give him the side-eye and note his nostrils flare in annoyance.

"I guess I'll have to quit playing around and *demonstrate* exactly how much of a man I am?"

"You're not a man, you're a demon."

His smile returns, much to my own annoyance. Followed by a chuckle that I feel right through me. "Fallen angel, actually, if you want to get technical. Call me a *demon* again and you might regret it." His lips press into a hard line, eyes staring ahead, smile vanished.

"Seriously, you're too..." I wave my hands around in exasperation. "You know... to be *The King*. Where are the horns? The red skin? The ugly face and forked tail and—"

Whirling on me, he grabs my chin, pulling my face close to his. I freeze like a mouse caught in a trap.

"I can show you that side of me if you desire, my Angel." His breath is against my mouth, and the pressure from his hold forces my lips to fall open. His tongue traces along my lower lip. I think I might die...

"Lessons begin in one hour. Don't be late," he speaks against my lips, and the world slips out from beneath my feet once again.

POSSESSED BY THE DEVIL

I rouse from a deep sleep, head foggy with an outrageous dream that I'm sure I was having but can't seem to grasp back again to examine. The stone beneath me is cold.

Such a relief! I'm not in Hell.

That was one crazy dream. The King and demon cities and Asmodeus.

Wait.

I shoot up. My head spins, so I grab the wall for support. If it wasn't real, then Asmodeus is still out there, and his ass is mine. Grinning, I move to find my backpack and weapons...

Nothing is where it should be. I can't find anything that's familiar. There are chains on the walls and bars on the door. I charge at it, yanking and shoving. It won't budge.

Motherfucker.

"You're dead, *DEMON*! You hear me? I'm going to cut your eyeballs out and send you to your own stinking pit!" I scream at the top of my lungs, and I swear I hear his answering chuckle whisper past my ear on a cool breath, but there's no one here.

Then, suddenly, there is. A woman stands outside my cell, wearing nothing but a silky camisole and thong. She's long and lean, with blond wavy hair that falls all the way to her ass. Big blue eyes, serene smile... the polar friggin' opposite of me.

"We don't have much time," she says. "Master wants you ready in twenty minutes. I thought you were never going to wake up. He'll be so mad if we're not ready. You need to wash and change, and I need to do your hair and—"

"*What* are you twittering about?" I grab the bars, pressing my face to them. She doesn't look like a demon, but we're in Hell, and they can be deceptive little shits.

"You have to be ready. Please don't try to fight me. There are guards. They'll punish you, then *he'll* punish you. And me." She unlocks my cage, takes my hand, and pulls me down a dimly lit corridor.

I'm so confused I don't even try to shake her off.

Besides, I can now hear the heavy footfall of those guards she spoke about following behind. I glance down at my body, but I can already tell by the way my clothes feel; none of my weapons are still in my possession.

I love that seraph blade. It's like a part of me, an extension of my body. If he's destroyed it—

"Here we are," the woman announces. "You need to strip and get in the bath."

"What's your name?"

She stares at me in a mix of incomprehension and irritation. "It's Jenna. But really, we have no need for names. I'm no one."

I snort. "I might try that. You know what it's like having to live with the name Angel when you're a demon hunter?"

Her eyes go wide as she looks from me to the guards lurking in the doorway.

"Yeah, don't worry, I'll take care of those guys soon," I whisper, offering a conspiratorial smile.

"Your words will get us both sent down. Please, do not speak anymore. You need to bathe, and I need to—"

"Sent *down*?"

Weren't we already down, technically? I mean, in theory at least. I don't think Hell really exists in the center of the earth. It's on some weird astral plane. But still...

"Please." Tears glisten in her big blue eyes, whipping me back to the moment.

"Okay, okay, chill out. No one's hurting you."

Not everyone in Hell is a demon or dead. I've been told that many of Hell's occupants are very much alive. *Wishing they were dead.* And Jenna appears to be in that category. I'd have sensed it by now if she was more than human. And not just because her eyes aren't black—because some demons can hide that—but because I find genuine fear on her face. A slight tremble in her hands.

I look around the room, and I'm hit by a terrible realization. All her prattling about bathing... this is a *bathroom*. There's a huge circular bath cut from the stone in the center of the room, surrounded by all manner of lotions and soaps. Hanging in the corner, an assortment of skimpy underwear.

"Oh, hell no." My head swings back and forth. "You are not preening and primping me like some piece of prized ass and presenting me to the Devil's bedroom. Fuck. This. Shit."

I step back into a wall of muscle. The demon hisses in my ear and shoves me toward the bath.

"He wants you to be clean and comfortable," Jenna says.

"Bullshit."

And that's when she starts crying.

Crying!

"What are you doing?" I reach out awkwardly to pat her shoulder. She just sobs louder.

"I can't fail. I'm already on a warning, please!"

The guards in the doorway laugh. I turn to see them cross their arms, thoroughly enjoying the show.

I'm supposed to do this with them standing there? Every instinct in me screams to fight. To stand my ground and defy the commands. But she won't stop crying. I can face a roomful of demons, no problem, but present me with someone crying and I want to shrivel up into a hole.

"All right." I sigh. "Just, please, quit the tears."

She stops instantly, making me dubious. Was that all an act? Hurriedly, she grabs some soap and gestures for me to get a move on.

Well, if I'm doing this, then I'm doing it my way.

Facing the guards, I slowly peel away my black vest and military cargo pants, kicking my biker boots off with a loud thud. One of them hits a guard in the shin, making him growl. I take my time with my bra and panties, loving the way their eyes bulge from their sockets and their hands ball into tight fists.

Turning around, I feel their eyes burning into me as I walk with an exaggerated swing in my hips and step into the steaming bath. It's too hot. My skin goes bright pink and my fingers tingly. My little assistant reaches for a jug. I bat her away. "Seriously, I'm doing this for you, but don't push your luck. I can wash myself."

She steps back in disappointment. I try to ignore her sulking as I scrub myself with something that smells like coconut and chocolate. It's weird. Not like the citrus stuff I usually use.

"It's nearly time," she whispers.

"Great. Let's get this over with." I dry myself and reach for my clothes, but of course she steers me to the lingerie section. With a heavy sigh, I grab the closest thing—some sort of black, lacy corset—and wriggle into it.

Honestly, could this day get any more fucking ridiculous?

⬢

IT TURNS OUT THE LEVEL OF RIDICULOUSNESS HAS BARELY EVEN begun.

After being herded through many stone corridors—lit by candles that don't seem to ever run down as there's no melting wax pooling beneath them—and up several sets of stairs, round and up and along and round and up, as if deliberately trying to disorient me, we finally arrive at the King's... what? His chamber? His office? What do you call the residence of the King of Hell?

Whatever it's called, the sight inside shouldn't surprise me, so it's annoying when a little gasp escapes before I can check myself. It seems damned obvious the more I think about it. Maybe the correct word is The King's *Brothel*.

Because there he sits on a throne, still only wearing jeans and boots, and draped in naked women—one of them sucking his cock through the open zipper. More of them surround the room, sprawled out like a photoshoot for the book *101 erotic poses*.

I refuse to let my eyes linger on the two chained up against a wall. Mouths gagged, nipple clamps, and vibrating things...

I've stepped inside one of those seedy BDSM clubs. *It's not entirely unpleasant...*

"I'd have expected a little more originality from the Devil himself," I mutter, picking my way past naked women to stand before his throne, wishing my gaze would stop landing on his abs. And that head bobbing in his lap.

His eyes track me from the moment I enter the room. A lazy smile hangs on his face. With a harsh snap of his fingers, the women around him retreat as one, like a flock of startled sheep, leaving just me and him in a weird, tense bubble.

Casually, while staring at me and licking his lips, he guides his solid cock back where it belongs. It barely looks like it'll fit—

"Why am I here?" I mentally slap myself away from thoughts of his dick. And there we go—that was the question I should have asked earlier. I almost pat myself on the back for not slipping out another comment about his ludicrously pretty face and chiseled abs... the lack of horns... the *size* of that thing...

Jesus fuck... my thoughts are like sloppy noodles.

He's still grinning at me, ignoring my question, and I start feeling the urge to squirm. I try to pull the corset up so that I don't have so much cleavage hanging out. I might be classed as petite, but my tits didn't get the memo.

"Well?" I press. "What was the big hurry in having me bathed and presentable? Is there to be a meeting? Are you selling me to the highest bidder? It seems a waste to go to all this trouble with coconut shampoo if you're just going to kill me."

I should be killing *him*, not jabbering on like an idiot. *Where's my blade?*

"You're mine." He shrugs, as if that's the most obvious answer in the world. "Where else would I put you but at my feet?"

I laugh.

He smiles.

"And what in your deluded little brain makes you think I'm *yours*?"

He leans forward over his knees, steepling his fingers beneath his chin, suddenly way more interested in the conversation. "Oh, I don't know, maybe this little thing called a *deal with the Devil*? Selling your soul to a demon. A demon pact. A Devil's bargain—"

"I have *never* sold my soul to a demon."

"No, but your father did. Only, it wasn't a demon that came to collect that day. It was me."

His words ring in my ears like hellfire itself is burning through my skull.

No.

Slowly, he leans back in his throne, satisfied with my response. My mouth hangs open, eyes wild with panic, but I can't seem to rein my face back in.

"He's already dead," I whisper. "Was it *you* that made him shoot himself? You already have his soul, you piece of shit."

"I never wanted *his* soul. I wanted yours, and he sold it to me."

"He wouldn't."

His eyebrows rise. "I've indulged you far too much, Angel. Get on your knees." He flicks his eyes down my body in disgust, suddenly tired of me. Switching from smiles to menace with alarming speed.

My feet root themselves through the stone. I growl in frustration. I'm armed with nothing but the tits spilling from my top and my sharp tongue. Somehow, I don't think these weapons are enough for taking on the Devil.

"Was I not clear enough? On... Your... Knees." A faint red glow forms in his black eyes.

"Fuck...You."

He nods, barely perceptible. "I can see you need a little more time to process all this."

He lifts his chin in a quick jerk and I'm grabbed from behind, my hands pinned into the small of my back. The guard drags me away. I struggle to keep facing the Devil, stumbling backward and staring him down. "You know I'm going to kill you, right?"

"I can't wait for you to try." He smiles.

Then, just as I'm pulled through the door, he calls out, "*Lucifer*. You can call me Lucifer."

I'M LED DOWN ENDLESS DARK PASSAGEWAYS, THE STONE COOL and crisp. It's not damp or dusty, just dark and ominous. It was swelteringly hot when we were outside. I can't work out why it's so cool in here. There are no air units buzzing. Is there even electricity in Hell?!

I try to make out anything that could be considered a landmark, some sort of way marker, taking a mental note of all the turns. I scrutinize every wall and door we pass for signs of escape routes, but there doesn't seem to be any rhyme or reason to the twisty route we're taking. I swear we've already gone around in two circles.

Eventually, I'm delivered back into the prison cell I woke to earlier. Except, this time, I'm not given the luxury of a nap on the floor. This time, my wrists are bound over my head, chained up to the wall before I can even blink, let alone retaliate.

Well, shit.

This is just getting better and better.

What the hell does he want with me? I know I'm pretty high up in the demon hunter ranks. I'd be a prized catch for many demons. They'd love the chance to break me. But the Devil? Surely, I'm just small fry to him. This makes no sense.

I don't believe his story about my dad for one minute.

My dad would have died before selling his soul, or mine. I rescued him once, after a hunt of ours went bad, and found him missing two of his fingers, most of his nails, and covered in knife wounds, burn marks, broken bones... those demons tried damned hard to make him rat out his hunter friends, but he didn't. He *wouldn't*.

He was a man of honor. He followed codes. And he hated demons with a passion that took over his whole life. Making a deal with the Devil would be the last thing a man like him would ever do.

Unless he was tricked into it?

No. He was too smart.

The chains above my head clank together as I yank them. My shoulders are already protesting in pain. There's nothing in this cell. Only the cold stone and the stink of hopelessness.

And that's not a thing I ever wallow in for long.

I'll find a way out of this, and when I do, I'm going to indulge in the greatest exorcism of my life. Sending the Devil into his own inferno will be pure gold.

CHAPTER SIX

It could be years since I was strung up like a prized idiot. Or it could be hours. I have no idea. Time seems to have blurred into a surreal notion. Is it passing at warp speed, or has it stopped entirely?

My head's foggy. My thoughts randomly switch from fantasies of bleeding Lucifer out by his throat, to running through a field of flowers like some hippy chick, chased by a giggling demon with ten-inch horns, calling out to me about how he's going to spank me when he catches me.

Am I awake or asleep?

The Devil looms over me, palming his cock, steering it toward my eager mouth—

"You ready to play nice now?"

My head snaps up, eyes springing open to find Lucifer standing right before me. His hand trails slowly from my navel, skirting past my breast, along my neck.

Hoisting myself by the chains on my wrists, taking all

my weight with an agonizing blaze that rips through my shoulders, I jump and smash my foot into his groin. He recoils, but quickly recovers, now with an extra dose of death in his eyes.

I should be afraid. But he's looked at me like this before... in my dreams... the threat of pain... the lack of mercy he'll show me...

My core thrums in approval, aching need between my thighs.

"You put those dreams into my head," I bark.

Angry at him. Angry at myself for loving them.

"No. The pact your father made *bonded* us. There's always been a connection. You just didn't know it."

"Seriously? How long are you going to keep up this act? Because I'm not buying it!" I click my neck, ready for him to dare touch me again. "Besides, I couldn't have known what you looked like unless you planted it there."

Jeez, woman, what does it matter? Bigger picture. Forget the sex dreams.

He steps closer.

Bring it, shit-sucker.

He pauses to assess me, just out of reach. "I assure you. I didn't plant those dreams. But you can go ahead and believe it if you like. It makes no difference to me. It's so much easier when there's someone else to blame for your darkness, isn't it?"

What? What darkness?

I find myself nodding.

Scrunching my eyes shut, I take a deep breath. "Are you going to kill me or torture me forever with this boredom? I mean, come on, being forced to bathe in delicious smelling products and chained up ready for kinky time? This is the best the Devil can do?"

Shadows unfurl behind him. Coiling blackness, drawing all the air from the room.

I will not fear the shadows...

I can't stop staring at the swirling dark, feeling sucked into it, my chest heavy as lead, ice in my veins. He suddenly seems ten times bigger than before. There's no way he just walked through that door. He wouldn't fit.

I bite my tongue, making it bleed. *Stupid mouth.*

Reaching out, corded muscles bulging with tension, he grips my upper arm. A thousand visions flash behind my eyes at the contact. My skin burns. It's on fire. No, it's pulsing with electrical current. It's too tight. I'm too hot.

I can't see.

There's just blood. And sex.

Whips and chains and knives and bodies and my head tipped back, writhing in sexual release. *I am the Queen of Sin.* It's too much, too quick, rapidly switching from one vision to the next.

I'm flying, floating away through the castle, dangling and dragged like a bunny in a dog's jaws... all floppy and scared and weak.

No, I'm not scared.

I want more.

I try to find the blood. I try to—

I land on the floor with a painful thunk.

Lucifer takes his throne, and I'm kneeling at his feet.

"Back here again!" I groan, swinging my head around

to find nothing has changed. There are still naked women everywhere, some engaged in sexual acts with each other, some sprawled about waiting for their turn.

I suppose I should be grateful the room isn't engulfed in hellfire with hooved beasts inflicting pain.

"This is where you belong, my Angel." The toe of his boot goes under my chin, lifting my gaze to his. I want to slap his foot away, recoil from the indignity, but his eyes are blazing red and, despite the calm posture, I feel his rage simmering under my own skin. It's as if my own dark energy is trying to reach his, eager to merge and ignite.

So, I let him keep his boot there, and I stare into those eyes, refusing to look away.

Perhaps this is a better way. Play along, be subservient so I'm not chained up again. Badass hunter I may be, but even I can't escape chains without help. But this way, I have a chance. Keep him sweet, gather myself back together...

"Escape is impossible, but I'm going to enjoy your efforts. Maybe I'll even let you, just for the pleasure of watching you crawl back to me when you realize the mistake." His boot drops to the floor. "Would you like to make your first attempt now or later?" His arms swing wide-open, gesturing around the room. "There's only one door, behind you, right across the hall. But you never know, you might make it if you sprint. I'm sure the guards will be no problem. Your blade is right here if you want it?"

My seraph blade magically appears in his hands.

Leaning forward, he presses the point to his wrist and slices upward in a swift, brutal movement. For a second, there's a hideous gaping wound, a flash of blood, and then the cut has healed.

Laughing, he tosses the blade, and it clatters in front of me. I snatch it up but remain on my knees.

"What do you want?" I try one more time.

"I want you to get up here and suck me off."

I choke on a cough before I can stop myself. Then I get to my feet, clutching the knife. Will his cock magically grow back if I *chop* it off?

I feel all eyes on me. The room is frozen in a held breath. Every woman staring at me, but what is that expression they hold? Jealousy? Fear? Anger? Do they want me to do this or not? Surely none of them *want* to be here?

"Let's not pretend you haven't already had me in your mouth many times." Lucifer absently strokes the growing bulge between his legs.

"You said you didn't plant those dreams."

"I didn't, but our connection gave me the same ones. Not that I sleep. It was more like visions—"

My knife hits him between the eyes, embedding into his skull. The exact same spot where I stabbed Asmodeus the first time. He'd reacted instantly, his blackened soul erupting from his mouth.

The women around the room let out a collective gasp of horror.

Lucifer releases a long-suffering sigh.

With all the patience in the world, he grasps the hilt

and draws the angel-blessed metal back out. After wiping the blood on his black jeans, he flips it around so he's holding the blade and hands it back to me.

I snatch it up.

My shoulders slump.

Shit.

This is going to be harder than I thought.

"As much as I'm excited to spar with you, Angel, you must know that misdemeanors cannot go unpunished." Lucifer rubs a finger over the healed spot on his forehead. "You're far too exquisite for the likes of the infernal dungeons, but don't think I won't send you down there for a little taster session if you don't develop some *give and take* in this relationship of ours."

I'm speechless. I rack my brain for a retort and come up blank.

"I've shown willing," Lucifer continues. "I gave you your blade and indulged you in your little fantasy for escape attempt number one. Now I expect something in return."

"If you seriously think I'm giving you a blow job—"

He waves his hand, cutting me off. "Bring him."

I flinch in confusion. Bring who?

A guard appears, shoving a man through the room to stand beside me. The man—no, the *demon*, glares at me suspiciously.

I recognize him but can't place it in my currently jumbled headspace.

"Come. Sit beside me, Angel. Get a *taste*." Lucifer pats a simple wooden chair that has magically materialized from the shadows beside him. I consider refusing, but there's really no point in fighting every single thing he says. *Pick your battles.*

Settling into the seat next to him, I'm all too aware of how I'm practically naked, but I don't feel it with my blade in hand. In fact, the only time I truly feel naked is when I'm stripped of weapons. Even though Lucifer has just proved how useless this knife is against him, I can't help gripping it tighter.

"Darius, I'm told that you're working with Lilith." Lucifer stares at the demon before us, and I can feel his dark wings forming against his throne, somehow there but not there, going right through it and spilling out behind us. The shadows swim in my peripheral vision.

Darius. Too familiar.

"N-n-no, my King, I would never." The demon shits his pants, head swinging in denial.

The very air itself buzzes with malicious fury beside me. Never mind Darius being scared. I can't bring *myself* to look at Lucifer. Just feeling his rage is terrifying.

"I don't give second chances, Darius. I gave you one opportunity to land yourself on the mid-level of the dungeon. All you had to do was man up and fess up. But now, you're going all the way down."

"No! No, please. I'll do anything." He tries bolting, even as he's trying to bargain, caught between the urge to flee and the hope of talking his way out of this. Suddenly, his body goes rigid. His mouth clamps shut. His eyes bug out so wide they might burst.

There's a strange gargling sound from his throat. The

veins in his neck thicken and darken, black snakes spreading through his skin, over his face. He can't breathe. Blood leaks from his nose.

Lucifer remains silent, but his wings have grown so huge that I can sense them overhead, dwarfing us, casting further shadow. Shadows that feel *alive*.

And then it comes to me. *Darius*. This is the miserable shit I'd summoned recently, the one who escaped.

"Angel, it's time to give back. I enjoy watching you in action. Finish him for me." Lucifer's voice has changed. It's rough, deep, animal... like two voices overlapping, something entirely inhuman.

There's no coincidence here, and I'm confused as fuck about why *this* would be what he wants from me, but I don't dare to look at him, let alone argue. Leaping from my seat, I ram my blade into Darius's heart without blinking. Killing demons is second nature. Doesn't even require thought.

He cries out, mouth yawning wide-open, but the blackened soul doesn't erupt like it should. He gags and coughs, *choking* on it. It won't come.

In resignation, I turn to face the Devil.

He grins, that boyish face all full of charm and impish delight, in total contrast to the devastatingly evil aura that permeates the air around him.

"Slowly, Angel. Let's take our time." He nods at Darius.

I turn back to the demon, who's still gagging on his rotten soul, caught between expulsion and being held in place. Lucifer is somehow keeping it inside him. Forbidding him to be exorcised so quickly. Drawing out the suffering. I can't even imagine the depth of power this must take.

For the first time in my life, I almost feel a little sorry for this hellspawn.

Almost.

I should be disgusted.

I should refuse.

I should turn and run.

I should do *anything* other than what I actually do.

But picking them apart slowly has always been my favorite hobby.

I will myself not to entertain Lucifer in this game, because surely it makes me no better than him? And indulging the Devil in his desires can only lead to trouble.

Yet my legs carry me, and my blade slices lazy paths over Darius's skin. He shudders and recoils as his soul tries so hard to escape the angel blade's wrath. It's stuck. Held there until Lucifer decides to release it.

And that power? This intense power that Lucifer possesses, that he's using for fun...?

My body sings in delight. Purring beneath his overpowering presence. Delighting in the torture I can bring to a demon. The darkness creeps in, clouding my vision, and I'm *lost*.

I'm gone, far away, to that special place where I feel whole. The only time I ever feel like I can really breathe. When I'm outside of my mind and body, and I'm just a machine. There's nothing but instinct and power and pain.

I'm vaguely aware of the women around the room, watching.

I want to kill them, too.

I want to kill *everyone*.

"Angel."

I'll bathe in their blood. I'll take everything...

Angel! Lucifer's voice cuts through the fog.

I glance from my bloody hands to the remains of Darius. His ruined body just a husk that once housed a demon. He's gone, but I don't remember it happening.

Lucifer is sprayed with blood. There's an arc that goes right along his impeccable abs—from his navel, upward, across his face.

I feel sticky. I know it's all over me too.

I want to straddle his lap. Lick his face. Suck his lips. Bite his neck. Grind myself against him.

He observes me like I'm the most wondrous thing in the whole universe.

The *Devil* is looking at me with barely contained awe. At the carnage I've wreaked. At the way my chest heaves with the thrill of it.

Shit.

My blade clatters to the floor.

CHAPTER
SEVEN

"*Well. That escalated fast.*" I rub a hand over my face, trying to remove the blood that's making my eyes stick together when I blink. I follow up with a little laugh to try and pop the tension in the air.

No one smiles back.

Except for Lucifer, of course.

His lazy, self-assured grin lights up that perfect face. Black eyes positively sparkling with humor. "My Angel, I knew you wouldn't disappoint."

I've always hated my name. But when the Devil calls me *his angel*, my insides dissolve into a heated, quivering mess.

"Don't get too excited. It'll be you I'm hacking to pieces soon enough." I quit smiling and clear my throat, finally noticing how inappropriate it is to show him any enthusiasm whatsoever. For once, though, my mouth doesn't want to stop grinning. I can't look at the mischievous smirk on his face without mirroring it.

So, I give up trying to hide my satisfaction from the kill. *Keep him blinded in awe of my sickness.* I stalk slowly forward, wondering how quickly I'll have to slice him up for it to halt his healing powers, enough that I can run—

"Don't spoil it, Angel." His voice deepens, almost to that point where it switches to several voices, all merged and terrifying. "I honestly don't want to send you all the way down for punishment and training, but test me one step too far and I'll break you."

My progress halts. I'm inches from his throne. He lounges in arrogance, slouched over his knees, studying me.

"You know, you keep making threats, talking the big man, but so far all you've done is prove to this room of sex slaves that all it takes is a little anarchy to make the Devil *weak* with desire."

His eyes flare red. My lips clamp shut, pulse rocketing.

Anyone would think I *wanted* his punishments.

I laugh nervously to myself.

Stop pushing. Stop pushing. Stop pushing.

Blood still rushes through my veins at a thousand miles an hour, the buzz from my kill flooding every nerve in my body.

"Or are you not *demon* enough for the task? Because, you know—"

"Did you just call me a demon? Again?"

I chew my bottom lip.

His wicked grin returns.

And I know, officially, without any doubt... I am one stupid motherfucker.

"Call me the Devil, call me the King of Darkness... fallen angel, sir, the antichrist. Hell, you can even mix me up with Satan if you must, but I am not a *demon*!"

He flips from amused to boiling over with fury in a heartbeat. Hellfire itself seems to dance in his red eyes. Malevolent. *Deranged*.

Lucifer doesn't employ his guards this time. Instead, he personally leads me through the tangled maze of corridors in his castle. He's not touching me, yet I feel his grip, like he's pulling me and there's no way I can refuse. He walks a step ahead, hands stuffed in his pockets. I try my hardest to dig my heels in, but I can't stop following.

Upward and upward, we climb higher. Which is new. And a relief. The infernal dungeon is *down*, right?

Wait, can't he just blink and materialize wherever he wants, dragging me with him? Like he's done before? All this walking is for some other purpose. Drawing it out. The *anticipation*... or simply a reminder of his power. That he can drag me along without even trying.

We remain silent during the journey. His rage simmers. Despite his hands being in his pockets, I can see the tension in his shoulders. The invisible leash he has on me pulses with promise and darkness and sin, stirring through the empty hole in my core, detonating thunder in my ears. It could be actual thunder. It could be my heartbeat. It could be self-preservation attempting to shut me down from the horrors that are to come.

Except, I don't feel scared.

I feel *exhilarated*.

We come to a large door. Pausing, it swings open by itself, and Lucifer steps aside, urging me to enter first. My feet move, even though I've seen something I can't comprehend inside, and I don't want to go. *I mustn't step through.*

I use every bit of strength I can muster to keep from walking. I manage to pause for a second in the doorway, then stumble, my legs and brain fighting with each other. I'm caught, only an inch away from certain death, knowing I can't fight it much longer.

This is it.

He's going to make me walk off the edge, into the gaping void ahead. Lucifer's version of walking the plank. There's no floor beyond the door. There's just a drop into the raging fire below.

Lucifer chuckles, sinister and low, the sound whispering all around me as he steps past into the pit. But he doesn't fall into the flames. He simply walks on air, suspended over the chasm. He turns to face me, holding out his arms. Floating there, with black wings vibrating behind him. Still coated in splashes of blood from my killing rampage on Darius.

"You won't fall in," he says.

I snort.

He releases his magical leash on me, and since I was resisting so hard the sudden loss of his pull has me falling backward, crashing to the ground.

"I swear to you, Angel. I won't let you fall. Take the

step by yourself."

Regaining my feet, I edge closer, peering down into the flames of Hell. It should be baking hot in here, but all I feel is cool air. I hold a hand out over the space, testing for heat inside the room. Still, only coolness.

I can't make sense of it.

I stare at him, unable to work out what exactly his big plan is here. Do I trust him?

Pfffft! I laugh at myself.

And yet, I'm curious, and I'm still buzzing with crazy energy, reckless and horny and *alive*.

I take a step, gently probing with my toe before putting any weight down.

My mind is instantly blown as I pass through, step after step.

I can't see any floor, not even one made of glass, yet I *feel* it. Solid as rock beneath my feet. I don't feel like I'm floating. I feel like I'm walking. Everything is normal—but there's a gaping, fire-filled cavern beneath me.

Lucifer chuckles again. Proud of his voodoo head-fuck. All of his earlier rage momentarily forgotten. I draw my eyes away from what's underneath and look up around the room. Along the edges, there are leather sofas, a table, a bar stocked full of bottles. I spin around in bewilderment. It's all too *normal* against the crazy below.

I gape at a window set in the dark stone wall and at the balcony, then through to the sweeping landscape beyond. I can see for miles. Beautiful black mountains under a red sky.

"Not what you expected?" he asks.

"Nothing about you seems as expected."

"Well, don't get too comfortable. You could have been relaxing with a whiskey in your hand, but you chose something different. And don't ever forget that. *You* chose it."

The feeling of solid ground beneath my feet dissolves. I scream, kicking and flailing. I'm suspended, still above the fire, but there's nothing to hold me up now. Only his will.

"Motherfucker!" I screech.

"I said I wouldn't let you fall, and I haven't."

My body hurts from the pressure of some invisible force holding me against gravity. The flames surge higher and they're suddenly *hot*. The heat licks my ankles.

I'm going to fall. I'm going to fall...

"You've been a very naughty angel," his voice deepens, several merged together. My skin prickles in warning. "I've waited so long for you. I hoped you'd show me more respect. That those dreams had already trained you in the behavior I demand. Did you learn nothing?"

Cocking his head to study me, he snaps his fingers, and my lingerie goes up in flames. I'm *literally* on fire, but it doesn't burn. I don't think I can say the same for the hellfire beneath me. My ankles scream in pain.

The fire on my body fizzles out. Flakes of ash rain down, as if whipped up by wind. And I'm naked. Arms and face still sticky with blood.

"I'm going to kill you," I mumble, forcing my legs to

stop flailing, relaxing into his invisible hold. *Deathly calm.*

Moments ago, I was exhilarated, arousal coursing through me at the idea of his punishments, craving the darkest things. Now, ice floods my veins despite the rising heat below.

I have no clue if this is a place to come for an orgasm or to die.

"Both." He shrugs. "Depending on who you are. And my mood."

"You can read my thoughts?"

"Sometimes. When you're riding high on the darkest part of your soul."

"I am *not* riding high on anything right now."

"No?" He levitates closer. His hand snakes behind my head, grabbing my ponytail and yanking my head back. His tongue samples the skin beneath my ear. Fingers swipe suddenly between my legs. "Then why are you so wet?"

I intend to kick him away in disgust. But what escapes my throat is a groan of pleasure.

A finger dips inside me. Briefly teasing. *Not enough...*

"Put your hands in the air," he whispers against my ear.

I don't move.

Mostly because I can't. My body has lost all coordination, and it's dark and dirty and sinful and exquisite.

I'm his puppet.
I'm his puppet.
I'm his puppet.

I whimper from the deep, delicious need inside.

He forces my arms up and I feel chains tighten around my wrists. I've no idea where they came from, or why they're necessary, since I'm already trapped, floating—

Where's my blade? A distant part of me wonders. The fighting part. The hunter instinct. I had it, before, when I did that demon, but then we were here, and I don't remember, and—

My gaze lands on his.

His eyes burn with new intensity.

"What do you really want with me?" I ask, hating the way my voice is all breathy with anticipation.

"You're mine. You will walk by my side."

"I'm a *nobody*. It doesn't make sense."

"You were promised to me before you were even born. I've waited *twenty-eight* years for you. You are far from insignificant."

I shake my head.

"Your father was human. He made a mistake. Is that so hard to believe? You think he was that infallible?"

Taking his time, Lucifer strolls to a table and returns with a strip of black material, toying with it between his fingers. He walks, but there's still no visible floor, and even the invisible one has fallen away, dangling me over certain death. Yet despite those shadowy wings, he still looks like he's *walking*... my brain is going to explode.

"My dad hated demons with a passion that ruled his life," I snarl.

"And where do you think that hatred came from?"

I open my mouth to speak, but no words come.

This can't be true.

The Devil nods. "Starting to come together now?"

It is, and it tastes rancid in the back of my throat. My whole life has been this messed-up murderous freak show, all because my dad sold my soul before I was born and then developed a demon-hating obsession?

I can't think about that.

Lucifer is still messing with the fabric in his hands, walking but floating, messing with *me*.

"So, you've been watching me since I was a *kid*, waiting to drag me back to this festering sex pit? That's disgusting. Creepy. Pervy. *Gross*—" He cuts off my tirade by pressing his lips to mine.

They're surprisingly soft. Pink and full. I don't remember much kissing from my dreams.

His tongue glides expertly against mine as his hand skirts up my inner thigh. Then he's pressing kisses along my jaw, sucking my neck, grabbing my ass.

"Gross," I mutter in weak protest, hips straining forward, eager to be touched at my aching core.

"Mhmmm," is his only response as he takes a step back and my whole body cries out in regret at the loss.

Come back! I bite my tongue against the plea on my lips.

I'm naked, sweating from the raging fire below, and that which burns through my insides on a tide of sinful fantasy. Breathing like there's no oxygen left in the world, dragging ragged gasps deep down into my disgusting soul.

I'll kill him.

I will.

But I can't do shit right now. Will it be so bad to have a little fun first?

Lucifer laughs. "Oh, my sweet little thing, you don't get to choose when the fun happens."

⁂

He leaves me dangling for eternity.

Until my mind starts to fray and snap from the anticipation, the desperation, the fear. I run through a thousand fantasies with all the ways I want to kill him, but each time my thoughts scatter and I end up fucking him instead of slaughtering.

"Okay, play time." Lucifer reappears with a smile. It's such a deliciously unnerving smirk. I can't work out if he's amused, angry, horny, or anything else. It changes every second. Cute and playful to wicked menace.

Still holding that strip of fabric, he lets go and it floats into the air. One moment it's hovering before me, then it's in my mouth, clinging tightly, *gagging me.*

Grunting, I try to convey pure hatred into the glare I give him.

Really, I'm mostly hating myself.

I could have fought harder. I could have protested more.

But I haven't, not really, because I *can't*.

I have an idea of what's coming, and I can't say no to something that I know is going to blow my mind.

I'm weak. Pathetic. Disgusting. Filt—

And oh my sweet baby angels what the fuck is that and I need more and holy fucking shit...

My head falls back, eyes closed, surrendered to the moment.

His lips close around my nipple, warm and urgent.

Rough hands knead my ass.

The skin over my hip stings as he bites it.

His tongue is in my mouth, claiming me.

Fingers are inside me, pumping in and out furiously.

My hair is fisted.

Hands curl around my throat.

Something vibrates against my clit.

All at once. *Everything*, all together, all the sensations, all the—

Just how many hands and mouths does he own? Has he transformed into a hideous creature? I don't want to open my eyes, but I do... and I find him observing me from across the far side of the room. Hands in his pockets. Jeans slung low. Bare-chested.

Smiling.

The sensations fall away. It felt so damned *real*! I glance down at my body, noting teeth marks on my hip. And the flames still dancing beneath me. Waiting to consume me.

I might welcome them. Before the Devil can shame me any further with my disgusting willingness to surrender to him. This is some messed-up voodoo shit.

Against my will, I rise higher into the air, pulled upward, away from the fire.

Then I'm falling, screaming, plunging into the pit—

My feet land against an invisible solid floor once more. I drop to my knees, staring down below. It's so deep, I can't see the bottom, but I get the dizzying feeling that the fire goes on and on, that you could just keep falling through the scorching heat *forever*.

I also feel *his* dizzying presence looming behind me.

I'm released. Now's my chance to try and disable him, to find a weapon, to run—

Agony flares across my ass, then over my back. The crack of a whip electrifies the air. Electrifies my body. *Fries my mind.*

The pain brings release. Takes me to the edge and drops me over, plunging into a dark place where I can breathe. *I like it here.* Each connection brings a sharp moment of hell followed by intense heaven.

But then it hurts *too* much. I don't like it anymore. I want it to stop—

I can't stand up. My knees are glued down.

I scream through the gag.

The lashings continue.

Years go past, every nerve in my body ignited, begging for release, but it won't end. There's pain and tingling and pulsing, and I'm atomic on the inside.

I can't take it—

I'm dragged into his arms. Hoisted up and falling into his chest. The gag falls away, dissolving into nothing. And I'm staring into the wicked eyes of my master.

I'll do anything he wants.

He releases me and I immediately drop back to my

knees. This time through my own volition. Somewhere along this road, he lost his jeans. He's naked too. I reach out to take his cock in hand.

Lifting a foot, he shoves my chest, pushing me back onto my ass.

"I'm the Devil," he growls. "You don't get to touch me. You worship on your knees, but you don't touch until I command it. Not until you're ready for the throne at my side."

I nod, dumbfounded. *Heartbroken.* I need to feel him. I need to taste.

He squats down. Clutches my chin between his fingers. He's so imposing. I feel as small as an ant, cowering from the way his eyes burn red.

I hate him.

I want him inside me.

"I like having you down here on the floor," he muses. "Maybe next time I'll lead you to my throne on your hands and knees. Your neck will look delicious with a collar around it. Pretty and tiny and breakable."

I hate him.

I want him inside me.

"You want the monster inside you?" His voice rumbles through the room like a megaphone. "Ask me for it, out loud. *Beg me.*"

"I don't beg." My voice is barely more than a cracked whisper. My throat hurts. Did he choke me? I think he did, but it's all so mixed up.

"We'll see about that."

CHAPTER
EIGHT

I wake up in *bed*.

Satin sheets and luxurious pillows. I groan as I stretch out my body, every part aching.

It hurts, and it feels so good, and I can't remember—

My eyes snap open.

Lucifer sits beside the bed, watching me with that lazy smile on his face.

Memories assault me. Just like my dreams. But this time, it wasn't a dream. It was real. Real, and yet not real, never certain if he was touching me with his body or his mind powers. And, oh God, I remember begging. I begged so hard, as if the world was ending...

I don't remember *it* ending, though. I don't remember how I got from clanking chains and buzzing vibrators and whips cracking, to sleeping in this incredibly comfortable bed. Peering over the edge, I'm relieved to find a solid black floor below. No more hellfire.

"You passed out." Lucifer's grin is infuriating.

"I did not!"

Did I?!

"It's nothing to be embarrassed about. You took way more than I'd anticipated for your first time."

"Shut up," I growl, pulling the covers up to my chin. I want to disappear into this fluffy haven of a bed and never come out. I'm clean. There's no trace of the blood that coated me before. I don't remember bathing.

"I'm serious. Your pain threshold is phenomenal. I knew you'd never disappoint, but this was—"

"I said shut the fuck up!" My face blazes with shame. This can't have happened.

I remember the pain. I can still feel it. My body feels like it's been run through a cement mixer for five hours.

But I also remember the pleasure.

The unearthly, out-of-this-world, insane *pleasure*.

"I thought you dealt *only* in pain," I mumble. "You got me off guard with voodoo floors and magical touches and—"

"You lie to yourself. You already know that pleasure and pain go hand in hand."

My eyes close as my head flops back in angry resignation. This cannot happen ever again.

"But you already know the pleasure I bring from your dreams, don't you?" he continues. Digging the knife in. Shattering the flimsy bit of self-respect that remains.

"Unless, what if they weren't dreams at all, Angel?" He won't shut up.

And this one gets my attention back onto his smug face.

"You said—"

"I said I didn't plant the dreams into your mind. Which is the truth because they weren't dreams. The *truth* is, I snuck you here into my castle every night to fuck you into oblivion, and then placed you safely back in your bed by morning."

"That's horseshit. You just spoke of me doing well for my *first* time." My eyes roll at his lame attempt at lying.

"Ah, but *which one* was the lie?"

My mind whirs with a thousand thoughts, but he's got me. How do I know which was the lie? The dreams always felt so real.

"Are we done here?" I fling the covers back and find my feet unsteadily. I wobble, trying to pretend I didn't... "You might have shown me the pleasure you can bring in your flaming room of pain, but are you about to bring me the morning-after pancakes in bed?"

Hands on my hips, I stand before him. Wondering what I'm hoping to achieve now.

Pancakes would be so damned good...

"Kneel for me." Lucifer nods at the spot before his feet.

I laugh.

"You don't have to go back to your cell. Kneel for me, outside of anything sexual. Pledge yourself at my throne, and you can be free to roam the castle. To sleep in my bed. To eat pancakes."

Free. No chains.

That will make escaping a butt-load easier. I can play

the perfect woman, indulge him, rest up... and then get the fudge out.

It's easy. I couldn't wait to get on my knees for him last night.

I saunter closer. Place myself toe to toe, looking down on him where he sits. A surge of adrenaline buzzes through me at the feeling of dominating *him*. I lean down and place my hands on his knees, getting face to face. His black eyes take on a lusty glaze. His smirk makes me shiver.

"Fuck. You," I whisper against his lips.

His face drops, serious and deadly.

Dammit! Stupid, stubborn tongue!

CHAPTER NINE

Am I *really* this stubborn?

Do I have an unbreakable need to deny authority at all costs?

Is my moral compass too strong to accept an offer from the Devil?

Or is it that I love making him mad? That, apparently, I can't get enough of his punishments?

Because we're now into the third time in as many days that he's fucked me raw, had me literally begging for more... and then I've turned around and told him where to go. Continued to reject his demands outside of the bedroom.

It's not a bedroom. It's a hellish burning pit of darkness and sin and pain. I should hate it.

Once again, here I stand, arms chained above my head in my shitty little cell, questioning my sanity. Jenna has been and gone. She fed me soup since she's under strict instructions not to remove my chains under any circumstances. I'm starting to quite like her. She doesn't talk much, but I feel like I connect to her on some level.

The guards leered at me for a while. Now, even they've gone.

All I hear is the occasional growl. The clink of claws on stone. I'm pretty sure there are actual hellhounds patrolling the corridors, and I sure as shit hope I don't bump into one when I eventually take a shot at escaping.

I'm cold. Alone. And confused as shit.

Nothing but wicked memories haunting my mind on endless loops.

Bent over his lap as he spanks my ass until it's numb.

On my knees begging him to take me.

Tied down to a bed and repeatedly fucked with a mechanical dildo until I'm screaming.

Orgasm after orgasm.

Torture and pleasure.

Pleasure and torture.

It's all so wrong. If he hadn't been in my dreams all these years, maybe I wouldn't be such a confused mess. It should be clear-cut. I can't lose sight of the fact that I'm a prisoner and he's a monster.

I just have to tell him I'm his. It doesn't even matter if I mean it or not. Just say the words and he'll release the chains and I can start forming a decent plan out of here.

I keep telling myself this. But the words he wants to hear won't come.

Maybe because if I say them out loud, I might start believing them too.

Lucifer keeps to his word.

It's time to make another appearance before his throne, and this time I'm leashed by a black collar around my throat. Nothing invisible. He wants everyone to see my subservience as I'm led to his feet on my knees.

I kinda like it.

I'm going to kill him.

"You're going to fuck one of my whores, right here, for my amusement," he drawls.

"Did you hit your head?" I look around incredulously. The women stare back at me, shifting their positions, as if hoping I'll pick them. I spot Jenna amongst them and can't help giving her a *'what the fuck'* look.

I snap my attention back to Lucifer, but he's already followed my gaze and is smiling at Jenna. "You'll do it, or *she'll* pay." He nods to her.

"You wouldn't." My jaw clenches.

A single eyebrow rises in challenge, but he's still staring at my meek little maid. "Tell me, girl, how did you enjoy your last punishment?"

Jenna's eyes widen in horror.

Part of me doesn't get it. Lucifer's *punishments* are something to seek out, not hide from. But I suppose they don't all get the same treatment I do. Or maybe I'm just *that* sick.

And right here, he knows he's got me. Is that why he always sent the same slave to tend to me? Because he knew I'd form a bond that he could manipulate?

No people-ing!

A guard drags Jenna forward and shoves her to the ground beside me.

No matter how much I hate people, no matter how socially awkward I am, I can't stop myself from stepping up and playing the hero, keeping others safe. My Devil stalker knows this too. He's no doubt watched me in action enough times.

It no longer matters that defiance boils in my blood. He's got me.

Well played, shit-stain.

"It's okay," Jenna whispers.

Like fuck it is.

I sigh, taking another look around at the options. I've never been with a woman before. Let alone been watched in the act. I'm suddenly filled with terror. It's one thing that my dreams involve the darkest, dirtiest shit, but the thought of kissing another woman, right here, right now, has me nervous.

Jenna takes my hand. I turn back to her, finding unusual determination on her face. "Do it with me," she says.

Lucifer chuckles.

I'm going to kill him.

"No, it's okay—" I begin, but she lurches forward and starts kissing me. It's uncoordinated, rough. I'm taken by so much surprise I can't figure out how to match her movements. But then she slows down, squeezing my hand, and we find synchronization.

She's so soft.

It's the most sensual kiss I've ever received.

I'm not here, in Lucifer's brothel—I'm in a meadow, surrounded by birdsong and summer sun and flowers. We're joined by the gentlest of touches. Her hands explore my curves, ghosting over my nipples, tracing paths down my spine, leaving tingles in their wake.

I need to touch her, too.

I've never needed something so gentle in my life.

There's no pain, no confusion, no darkness—she's the sun and I'm pulled into her warmth.

I discard my skimpy underwear and pull hers away. We're still in a meadow, or a beach, or a forest. Somewhere romantic. There's nothing else in my vision but her. She's staring at me with nervous anticipation. Suddenly, her touch has given *me* confidence.

I guide her slowly onto her back, running kisses up and down the length of her body. Trailing my tongue over her softest parts, marveling at the feel of a full fleshy nipple between my lips. Her little groans of pleasure are intoxicating.

Eventually, I settle between her legs. Blowing, sucking, licking. She's some sort of delicious meal and I'm ravenous, ready to take everything on offer. I keep going until her squirming turns into an abrupt shiver, gasping, clenching, pulsing.

Then I'm on my back and the sensation between my own legs is nothing short of wondrous. I can't see anything other than her, fascinated by watching her as she pleasures me—

Everything goes pitch-black.

Only for a moment.

Then I'm hovering over infernal hellfire and Lucifer is pacing angrily up and down.

"You stole my orgasm!" I yell.

"I changed my mind. You're not for sharing."

"You're jealous." I can't help smiling.

"I don't know what to do with you. I can't work out how I want to treat you... you're *different*. It's all new." He scrubs his fingers through his hair.

"And confused!" My grin spreads wider. *I've flummoxed the King of Hell!*

I watch, fascinated by the sight of this powerful monster as he marches up and down. I've never seen him pace before. Stalk, like a caged lion waiting to attack, yes. But anxiously pace? No.

Finally, he stops. Drags a deep breath. Turns to face me.

And there he stands, waiting, as if expecting me to hold his answers.

I shrug, still grinning, enjoying this way too much.

"Pledge yourself to me, Angel." Lucifer uses his calm, nice-guy voice as if he's asking me to pick up some cookies from the store, not commit myself to Hell and all its debauchery.

"What does it matter? I'm *sold* to you. You already have me, anyway."

"That may be true, but I won't offer you any freedom at all until you admit what's inside your heart and say it out loud."

"Like a confessional?" I ask.

"Sure," he replies slowly, eyes narrowing.

I'm still dangling over the fire. Naked. Amused by his confusion and *angry* at the same time.

"Great! I've been desperate to get this shit off my chest." I smirk. "When I was five, I pretended to my dad that I hadn't seen him crying like a baby over a photo of my mom, and then, when he was charging around in a fit of rage two days later because he couldn't find the photo, I pretended I hadn't seen it even though I'd taken his lighter and burned it because I didn't want to see him like that ever again."

Lucifer just stares at me, nothing on his face.

"When I was nine, I broke a girl's nose at school for calling me a freak. Then, when my dad was about to kick my ass for breaking rules and hurting a *human*, I told him she'd said that my mom was a whore. He just walked away with more sorrow in his eyes, and I didn't get my ass whooped."

His shadows spread behind him, flickering.

"When I was fourteen, I snuck out of our apartment when Dad passed out drunk, just so I could single-handedly take on a demon he'd been watching. I wanted to see what his blood tasted like and knew Dad wouldn't approve, would never let me if he was there."

"Enough," Lucifer warns.

"When I was little and used to get scared of the shadows, I would think about murder as a distraction. Instead of thinking about nice fluffy things to calm me down, I'd think about how long it takes to bleed someone to death, about how it feels to cut them up, about the way a demon's blackened soul sometimes lingers mid-air before vanishing."

"Angel." Lucifer's eyes glow red.

"When I was sixteen, I told my dad I was done with being a freak, done with his shitty lifestyle, just *done*—with enough childhood trauma to keep a shrink busy for years. I walked away." I blow out a breath. "A year later, I realized that no amount of time-out could fix the monster inside me. I returned to him on my seventeenth birthday. An hour too late because he'd just blown his own brains out."

I want Lucifer to let me fall into the pit right now. Buried guilt resurfaces with a crushing blow to my chest.

My mom died because of me.

My dad died because of me.

Dad would be ashamed if he could see me now. The way my body craves the Devil's touch. The way I can't help but want to find out just how low I can go, just how sick and twisted I could become with Lucifer's touch on my skin.

"I told everyone at school that Santa was really a demon and that when they went to sleep, he was going to come into their rooms and take their eyeballs as gifts for his elves. I've never shed a single tear for the fact I never knew my mother. I've always avoided relationships because I enjoy breaking things and I might break *them*. I've spent my whole life waiting for the shadows to claim me, and now they have and it's a... huge... fucking... anti-climax."

I drag the biggest breath into my burning lungs.

Tears prick my eyes.

My hands tremble.

Lucifer blinks, then my back is pressed to the wall and his lips crash into mine.

After a split second of darkness, the room has shifted again, and we're in a *normal* room—one with black stone walls and a solid floor.

A floor that bites into my back as he presses me down; looming over me, naked, shadow wings curling behind him with wicked points that spike out from the tips. An occasional glimpse of onyx feather through the dark that coils around him.

I reach for his chest. He grabs my hands and pins them above my head.

And now his whole body is connected to mine; his chest against my breasts, erection between my thighs, lips hovering over my own.

We're on pause.

Frozen.

Breathing heavy and fast.

Connected and aching and desperate to take something from each other. Something the other doesn't want to relinquish.

"You can't have me," I whisper, lips brushing his and igniting every lustful nerve.

"I've had you your whole life." The head of his cock nudges at my core with building pressure until he gently slips inside. My breath catches in my throat. I'm burning up with the riot of *need* to have him claim every part of me. To submit everything I am and surrender to the wicked oblivion he promises.

He doesn't play fair. If he hadn't been in my dreams for so long, I'd stand a better chance against this sordid lure. But he's right. He already has me. I was addicted before I ever really even *tasted*.

My hips lift, urging him deeper still.

"I hate you," I moan.

But as he thrusts with increasing pace, the fight drains out of me like butter on a hot knife, slipping away.

He's so painfully *hard* inside me. Every part of him is all toned edges and solid muscle, defined to the point of perfection. There's not a single ounce of softness anywhere. Except, sometimes, his lips—the only tender part of him.

He releases my hands, and they immediately find his back, nails dragging down his skin, drawing blood. His wings are there but I don't feel them. Approval hums from deep within his chest, pace increasing, driving into me with a new frenzied force.

I've had you your whole life.

My whole life. Waiting for the shadows to take me. Imagining all the horror that would come. How maybe it would be better just to follow in my dad's footsteps and end it all before it could begin.

I will not fear the shadows.

They fill the room, coiling and swirling, a mass of darkness with only one intention; to consume me.

And, oh, how my body wants that.

I'm so tiny in his magnificent presence. Humbled. *Owned.*

Jet-black eyes bore down on me. There are no whites to them, just this oppressive coal. Sometimes they're slate gray or flaring red, but usually it's this sparkling darkness, like glitter thrown into black ink. Beautiful in an unfathomable way.

"Tell me you're mine, Angel." His voice is rough, strained. He's hanging on by a thread. And when the Devil snaps, there will be no mercy.

"I belong to no one."

He stills. Completely motionless, erection throbbing inside me.

I wriggle for more.

He's a statue.

"Fuck you!" I cry, grinding harder, thrusting my hips up and down so that I'm fucking *him*. He pulls out, only the tip teasing my entrance, rendering my thrusting useless. Holding his considerable length, he slowly swipes up and down, spreading my desire all over, painting me with the evidence of my need.

"Fuck me!" I scream.

He leans down, breathing into my ear, nibbling my neck. "If you don't need me, get up and walk away."

Get up. Walk away.

So simple.

I shake my head.

Pulling back, he smiles, but there's disappointment in his eyes. Angry that I haven't walked away? Or angry that I still won't say those words?

He slams home, burying deep. My back arches, shoulder blades scraping against rough ground. But I resist the urge to close my eyes and stare right through him, trying to find any trace of humanity in those black orbs of his.

His gaze narrows, mouth parted with his own pleasure.

The next thrust makes me cry out, brutally claiming me underneath his powerful body.

I don't blink.

He grabs an ankle and hoists my left leg over his shoulder, stretching me to the point of pain.

Slam!

He rocks into me so hard that my head lifts and then cracks into the rock beneath me. I bite my bottom lip by accident, drawing blood. His demonic gaze narrows as he focusses on my mouth, nostrils flaring like he's some vampire desperate for a taste.

A grin creeps over my face as I lick the crimson essence and savor the metallic tang on my tongue.

"Is this all you've got today?" I prod the beast. "Oh dear, *Daddy* Lucifer is off his game. Did my emotional outburst rattle you? Maybe—" My own gasp cuts me off, and from here on I can barely breathe, let alone talk.

The inhuman pace he sets is relentless. The only pause is when he manhandles me into another position. One minute I'm on my back, sinking through the black stone and floating away on tides of delight, then I'm on my knees, screaming as they're shredded against hard stone from his onslaught.

With a hand around my throat, he hoists me up until my back is flush with his chest and I'm teetering, balancing on those grazed knees, knowing I'll topple straight onto my face if he lets go. But he doesn't. He keeps me pinned against him, teeth tugging my earlobe, hands tightening and tightening around my neck as he spears into me over and over.

When my vision blurs and I'm about to clock out from lack of oxygen, he loosens his hold just enough for me to gasp. Then his fingers curl and tighten once more, choking me into delirium, my head swimming with dizziness as my body tingles and spasms from toes to scalp.

Each time I come close to climax, he shifts position.

Starts over again.

His shadows fill the room, so much that I can barely see a thing.

There are no whips this time. No chains or toys.

The only weapon is his *stamina*, which he uses to completely destroy me.

CHAPTER
TEN

HE HASN'T SENT FOR ME IN DAYS.

Lucifer's new form of torture is to *abstain*.

Leaving me here; alone and needy. It's killing me. And I bet he fucking knows it.

So, I'm delighted when a momentary shadow appears outside the bars of my cell. Then it's inside and Lucifer is here with me, without needing to open the door. Normally, he sends guards when he's ready for me.

"Finally!" I breathe. "Are we slumming it in the cells for kinky time now?"

He doesn't look at me the way he normally does, with lust and anger and awe. He doesn't look at me at all. He simply sits on the stone floor, back against the wall, dragging his hands through perfectly styled, blond hair.

"Bad day at the office?"

He laughs bitterly. "No more than usual."

What is he doing? *Stand up!*

He heaves a sigh. Stares at his feet.

Seriously. Are we about to make small talk?!

Oh...kay. I'll run with it. "How long, exactly, have you been doing this... *job?*"

"Do you ever tire of hunting?" he fires back.

"Never."

He nods thoughtfully.

"Do you tire of screwing people over?" I ask.

He *looks* tired. There's strain on his face, dulling his sparkling black eyes.

"Never." He offers a smile to the floor, but it's not the usual dazzling one.

This is weird.

Lucifer sits on his throne, stalks his castle, owns my body with those eyes blazing and wings wisping behind him. *Death in his eyes and ecstasy in his touch...*

He does *not* sit like this. It's so disarmingly alien to see him sitting on the floor, looking like an ordinary man. Okay, not *ordinary*, but there's something vulnerable in him like this. Something that makes him more human, more relatable. And damn if my stupid heart doesn't ache for him to tell me why.

"Your father made a deal and sold his soul when he was just eighteen years old." Lucifer picks at a thread in the torn knee of his jeans.

My jaw clenches. *Goodbye* sympathy.

"Only, he didn't sell *his* soul," he continues, and my teeth grind. "He thought it was all a bit of a laugh during the demon summoning. Him and his buddies ready to sell their souls if they could only get the whole cheerleading squad to fuck them in a mass orgy. They were drunk, messing around. Your father didn't realize that one of his friends actually knew what he was doing with the summoning spell. Or that the Devil himself would show up."

I don't want to hear this... I don't want to hear this...

"He sobered up fast when I appeared. I wasn't much interested in the others, but your father was different. There was this aura, this sense of something bigger. I gave him a choice—his soul in ten years' time, or that of his first-born child, which I'd collect on her birthday."

"You're an asshole."

"I never said *which* birthday, of course." Lucifer still picks at his jeans, looking too human, almost apologetic. "He assumed I meant the actual day of birth. When I never came on that day, he relaxed for a while. Then he became increasingly anxious with each passing year."

My dad sold my soul to have a fucking orgy?!

"I hate you." I'm not sure if I'm talking to the Devil or my dad.

"He never expected to have a child, thinking he could play me. He made the deal with zero concern because he never planned to have kids, so there you go, job done. The Devil had been *tricked*. What a clever guy. He was so smug."

My jaw clenches tight.

Lucifer lets out a short, sharp laugh. "I'd never have made that deal if I didn't already know the child he was destined to have. The vision had pressed behind my eyes. The idea of *you* felt unlike anything I'd experienced before."

A single, silent tear leaks from my eye, tracking down my cheek.

He still hasn't looked at me, and I don't want him to. The next time those demonic eyes meet mine, I'm going to explode in rage.

"He loved your mother immensely, but he was furious when she got pregnant all those years later. She'd assured him she was on birth control. Even so, he was obsessed with precautions and always wore protection. She whined at him relentlessly that he didn't need to, but he never listened. Until one night when he was so wasted, he let her talk him into it. And that was all it took."

He pauses.

Clicks his neck from side to side.

Scrubs his face.

"She never knew about his deal, of course. And she always wanted a baby. She timed her deception perfectly with her cycle. She was never on birth control."

My head swings. My heart cracks for the mother I never knew. I've always loved her, believed her pure and good and everything I'm not. Why would she do that?

She died when I was a baby. Killed by demons. Dad tried to protect her, but he was knocked out.

More tears. Now they stream down my face.

"He didn't succeed in protecting her from the demons that came to kill her, not because he was overcome and outnumbered, but because he *summoned* them. For a new deal. Her life instead of yours."

He looks at me now, and it all fractures. My heart, my mind, my soul.

"Despite the deception that bore you, he fell in love with you the moment you came along. He'd have done anything to protect you. Of course, the demons agreed. But they were in no position to make such a deal. You are mine, Angel, and nobody has a say in what's mine."

I can't see him anymore. Floods of silent tears blind my vision. My head drops.

"Your father realized pretty quickly that the deal was fake. That's when he took to running. And hunting. He'd already formed connections with hunters from before you were born, he sought them out immediately after our deal. But his life's mission to build you into a warrior, strong enough to defend herself, began when he lost your mother."

"When I was four years old, I used to hide under my bed when I was left home alone because *Daddy* was out hunting." My voice is barely a whisper. "Do you know what it does to a four-year-old kid to know that the monsters in the shadows are *real?*"

He doesn't answer.

"Dad would yell at me when he got home if he found me hiding. I wasn't allowed to be afraid."

"I know. I was there. In the shadows."

Of course he was. He *was* the shadows.

A sob explodes from my throat.

"He was right. You needed to be strong. We both played our part in making that happen." Lucifer shrugs.

"So many times, I doubted my sanity... but I was

right. I *knew* the shadows were alive! Didn't you have anything better to do than haunt my sorry ass?"

"I wasn't haunting, stalking, or being a sick perv. I was watching out for you. *Protecting you.*"

"Pfffft! It's you I need protecting from!" I throw my head back, looking up at the chains binding my hands.

"Those are only temporary," he mumbles.

Mumbles!

He's never sounded anything but commanding before.

"So why did you wait so long? If you were watching me all that time? I don't believe you have a single atom of morality in your body, but if you were waiting until I'd reached sexual maturity to claim me, you could have done it long ago. I've been banging guys for years. You let them sully what was yours?"

I'm desperate to hurt him while he's looking so vulnerable. To say something that will make him rage, so that he'll get up off that floor and flood me with *real* pain. His own brand of exquisite release. Stop sitting there and spilling his confessions and *fuck* me already. Take it all away—

"I enjoyed watching you in action, honing your strength, fueling your bloodlust. I have eternity. I could wait until you were truly ready."

"Well, congratulations, Lucifer. I *am* ready. Soon, I'm going to kill you." My vision clears. Our eyes meet.

There's no smirk. No cocked eyebrows. No retort.

He just sits there looking like the boy next door with his perfect hair, sun-kissed skin, and uneasy body language; like a teenager about to ask Dad if he can take me to prom.

He's a monster. *Of the worst kind.* The sort that wears fake skin, looking beautiful and normal and somehow making me feel bad for him while he talks of all the shit he's caused *me*. Creeping in through my defenses with expert prowess.

His silky-smooth bare chest rises and falls with heavy breaths. He's always shirtless. I've never seen him clothed other than low-slung jeans and boots.

"Do shirts get in the way of your wings?" I ask.

No more talking about Mom and Dad or my shitty childhood. I swallow it all down. There's no time for wallowing and Hell is a dangerous place to start falling apart, right where the vultures linger.

He looks surprised. The slightest quirk to his eyebrow. Amused by the change of conversation. "What?"

"Just wondering why you never wear a shirt."

Finally, he smiles. It's a relief. And I hate him more for it. "No, clothes don't stop them. They defy the laws of physics."

"Oh, it's as I suspected, then. You really are just an egotistical dick. Parading around, *sans* shirt, to remind every other guy how insignificant they are next to you? Have all the girls dripping with need."

"I don't need to flash my abs to have that effect, my love."

My love.

My mind stutters. Trips. Short-circuits.

"Would you stop doing that!" I yell.

"Doing what?!" He chuckles.

"Sitting there like you're a man and not a monster. *Talking* to me. Just stop all of it!"

"Okay. Go ahead and let me know what you want right now, and it's yours." He pushes gracefully to his feet. Steps up to my dangling body. Damn if these chains aren't *killing* me. Everything aches. Not in a good way.

"Well?" he urges, the pad of his thumb sweeping over my dry lips. All traces of vulnerability vanished. "What do you need?"

You.

Your body.

Your punishments.

Your tongue.

Your hands.

Your shadows.

Your everything.

"I need you to get the fuck out of my cell."

And *poof!* Just like that, he's gone.

CHAPTER
ELEVEN

I'M BACK TO BEING ALONE. ENDLESS DAYS AND NIGHTS THAT blur into one long train of misery.

The only time I've felt remotely happy since arriving in Hell is when I'm actually *with* the Devil. But I keep pushing him away.

I'm on minimal food and water, naked, with a bucket beneath me as a toilet. Jenna graces me with a daily bath and some soup. Lucifer sure knows how to romance a lady.

But even if I was hungry, I couldn't eat. I've had time to let my thoughts run wild and I'm becoming increasingly panicked by the fact that the *antichrist* fucked me without protection. Can he get me pregnant? What sort of demon spawn could I be harboring?!

And in addition to that, something has shifted. I can feel it in the air. In the way the guards behave. Something is happening out there, and it kills me not knowing what.

When I'm finally released from my chains and delivered to Lucifer's quarters, I find a very different man than the one who sat in my cell. I don't even have time to let out some snarky remark before the invisible floor falls away and I'm dangling, barely away from the flames, heat and pain striking like asps.

I can barely contain my relief. He'll make it all stop now. He'll take it all away with his wicked lips and his gigantic—

"Going to your cell was a mistake," he growls, magically securing my hands and ankles with bonds I can't see, but I can feel them like heavy chains holding me still. Bent over at the waist. Legs spread. Arms pulled out in front of me, keeping me from straightening up.

"I let my guard down and you gave zero respect in return. That cannot go unresolved," he adds.

Yes, Master, I want to say. I bite my tongue.

His chuckle turns my relief to dread.

"Your time for pleasure has been and gone, Angel. I'm done pandering to you. It's time you saw a different side to me."

He steps in front, and I have to do a double take. A faint red sheen emanates from his skin.

"You're glowing!" Not for the first time, I'm mesmerized by the sight of him.

"Sometimes it slips through." His voice is rough. "You bring out the worst."

"Show me."

"No."

"I want to see. *All* of it."

"You don't."

"Do I look like some weak-ass bitch who can't take it?" I yell, then scoff at myself for the way I'm positioned at his mercy.

He stoops down, peering into my eyes. I fall into his, which are blazing brighter like his skin. "Some mortals go insane from the vision of my true form. Their mind breaks—"

"Get over yourself. You're not *that* mind-boggling! They probably went insane from the torture, not your pretty face."

Push him, push him, push him.

"One day," he muses before stepping back and snapping his fingers.

A whip appears in his grasp.

Not the flogger type that bites then caresses.

The evil type that looks like it'll strip my flesh.

My mouth slams shut.

"Do you know how long it takes to die from whipping alone?" His face is something primitive, and I don't want to look, don't want to see whatever sick shit is brimming out through every pore. "Because I do, Angel. You could say I'm an *expert*."

He drifts closer, too close, his body a flame next to mine. "You've disappointed me, my love. So, this will end when you start being honest with yourself and make the pledge to my throne," Lucifer whispers against my ear, right before the first lash makes me scream.

CHAPTER
TWELVE

He switches from man to monster in a second.

I hate it. I love it. Then I hate myself for loving it. And I hate him... and round and round I go. My fucked-up little merry-go-round. *The Devil loves me. The Devil loves me not. I love the Devil. I love the Devil not.*

Am I really this sick? Am I a terrible person? Am *I* a monster? Do I switch from one to the other with the same speed he does?

Yes. I do.

I can't stay here. My feelings for him are because he's in my head and under my skin and Hell has this weird dark energy that gets into my blood and makes it sing for more.

I need to get away. Once I'm out from under his twisted spell, then I can get my shit together. Do my job. Hunt him. *End him.*

Kill the Devil and move on.

CHAPTER
THIRTEEN

Jenna continues tending to me each day. She brings meager food rations. Bathes me. Dodges my sarcasm and angry tirades with wringing of her hands and muttered apologies. She refuses to talk about what went down in front of Lucifer's throne. I've complimented her numerous times on the quality of her kissing. She always looks like she'd rather the floor dissolve and sink into the pit than listen to another word about our encounter.

It was so surreal. She showed me the pleasure in a gentle touch, something my dark soul doesn't generally look for. The whole thing was like an out-of-body experience. Maybe it was Lucifer using his mind fuckery to seduce me into performing for him. Maybe she has magic tits.

I can't work her out. She seems too pliant, so nervous and shy, but then she did that with me? There's something more in her eyes. She won't look at me for long enough to analyze it.

"So, what's it like? You know, *down below*?" I whisper with exaggerated awe as Jenna busies herself picking up the lingerie I dumped in front of the guards. I've come to know them now as Luke and James. Their ridiculously normal names crack me up. I like to tease them often.

"Please, don't talk about it." She scoots past, ushering me to the bath, since I'm just loitering around naked. Her eyes cast a quick glance at the bruises on my wrists, and I know she's already gaped at the welts on my back from Lucifer's whip.

In truth, I'm not stalling to wind up the guards with my nakedness, but because that water is going to sting like a *mother*fucker.

"That bad, huh?" I press.

She takes my hand and leads me silently to the scalding water. I finally get in, wincing as I lower myself inch by inch. "Seriously, though, is it all hellfire that burns you for eternity? Beasts and torture and endless—"

"Stop!" She crouches to my level, staring into my eyes with an entirely new boldness. Or is it desperation? "Please," she mutters, recomposing herself, moving away. "It's believed that if you even *mention* it out loud, Master will hear and send you down."

I blow a breath as I lean back and soak aching muscles. "He won't send me down. I'm *far too exquisite*."

"And lies drip from his tongue like falling rain."

"What was that?" Luke asks, stepping toward Jenna. I don't like the look in his eyes. Or the tone of his voice. Hairs rise on the back of my neck.

"What?" She backs away.

He keeps coming. Right into her face. "Did you just call your King a liar?"

"N-no." She staggers as he grabs her throat.

"Hey!" I'm out of the bath in a flash.

Luke pins her to the wall. I reach instinctively for a weapon, every nerve fired up, ready to destroy him.

I'm naked. Soaking wet.

I slip on the floor as I lunge for him and land on my knees. His laughter rattles through my skull.

"No one speaks against the King without paying for it." James joins Luke as they shred Jenna's clothes from her trembling body.

"Then punish *me*, shitheads! I pushed her. I made her talk out of turn. You know she'd never do something like that normally."

They totally ignore me. Luke gropes her. James unbuckles his pants.

The spark I sometimes see in her eyes is gone. Hazed over. She goes limp in resignation.

"Oh, I get it." I stalk up behind them. "You like them weak and vulnerable. You're too afraid to take on a fighter. That's cool. It's not everyone's cup of—" As I turn away, hands grip my hair, yanking me back.

"You think you can fight us, little human?" Luke presses in behind me.

"I can hardly wait," I breathe, right before thrusting my head back into his nose. The crunch is so satisfying, I grin like a maniac. I've waited too long to deal with these dick-weasels. "If you want to get back to her, you'll have to go through me first. Let's play, boys."

As they fling me against the far wall, I glare at Jenna, urging her to leave. She stands, conflicted. Only for a moment before making the correct decision and running. I'll keep them distracted for an hour or two. Hopefully, they'll forget all about her and move on to a new game by the time a new day dawns.

Two minutes in and I hate to admit it, but without my weapons it's a little ambitious taking on two demon guards; ones strong enough to have landed a job in Lucifer's castle. I manage to throw some punches and kicks, but ultimately, I can't keep them at bay for long. It happens a lot quicker than I'd hoped for.

And as I'm bent over, Luke behind me, James at my face, ready for a hellish spit-roast; I have to question the sanity of this idea.

"Let's find out if you taste as sweet as a real angel." Luke plunges into me, just as the walls shake and the room goes pitch-black.

There's a deep, thunderous rumble that has the stone beneath my feet vibrating, and over the top of that I hear their yells for mercy. Disorientated, I stagger into a wall in the dark.

"Please, my King..." His voice trails off into an agonized yell and the crunching of bones. The wet slosh of blood.

A twisted thrill ignites my core.

Gradually, my eyes adjust. Or the darkness fades.

And there stands Lucifer, looking nothing like a man,

his skin *blazing* red. Not the subtle glow I'd seen before, but bright and furious. His boyish face something beastly that I dare not examine. Horns on his head and black claws for nails.

James is a bloody pulp at his feet. I can't even work out what's happened to him. He's just a gloopy broken mess.

Luke falls to his knees, head bowed. "Forgive me."

Lucifer looks at me and I freeze.

This is so very bad. He wasn't wrong. I don't want to see him like this. It's terrifying. Is he going to turn me into the same pitiful pile of blood and bone?

"They were defending your honor. Isn't that what you pay them for?" I offer, eyes to the floor.

I'm met with silence, which eventually forces me to look up. His head cocks. He studies me with a supernatural stillness about him. And gradually, his skin fades to its normal tanned state. His face softens. The horns disappear. The stone walls stop rumbling and shaking. Shadows retreat.

But his chest still heaves with anger.

"Please," Luke cowers on the floor, mumbling over and over.

Lucifer returns his attention to him. He raises a hand slowly in the air, and the guard is lifted. His hulking body hangs in the air between us. Face the perfect picture of terror. I can't help feeling a little happy about that.

Still, as much as I enjoy inflicting pain on demons, I'm not ready for what happens next. For the way Lucifer toys with him, casually breaking bones and tearing skin; for such a long time that I wonder if it will ever end.

The King of Hell is brutal.

Savage.

Breathtaking.

I've never witnessed such power. Such raw carnage.

By the time he's finished, Lucifer's skin is red once more, only this time it's not glowing, it's glistening from the blood that drips all around. He hasn't looked at me in eons, but now he turns, squares up to me, shadows pooling lazily behind him. There's a new calm in his eyes. He looks... *satiated?*

I've never felt so naked. Okay, yes, I *am* naked, but I'm more exposed in this moment than I'm comfortable with. I feel like he's seeing right into my soul. That he can sense how my sick heart is racing with sheer excitement for the beast before me. How the throbbing between my legs intensifies with each second that I'm pinned under his deadly glare.

"So then." My voice is hoarse. "Don't like people playing with your toys?" I try to lighten the mood, nodding to the remains of the guards. Although Luke now seems to be in several places.

Sheesh, it's suffocating in here.

Too dark, too deadly, too demented.

There's ringing in my ears and my blood blazes with wild fury.

"Did it turn you on?" he asks, still a little of the ragged inhuman quality that comes out in his voice with anger. Or excitement.

And yeah, he's excited. I can see it bulging through his jeans, which are ripped and torn into tatters, barely clinging to him by threads due to the *size* he grew to in beast mode.

"You're crazy," I whisper.

My stomach flip-flops.

"Probably." He nods. "But that's not relevant here."

I step away because he's stalking toward me, and I know what's coming and I shouldn't *want* it.

"You can't hide your arousal from me, my love, I can feel it from a mile away."

"Don't do this to me."

"Do what?"

"Don't make me a monster like you." I want to cry. I want to scream.

I want to *fuck* him.

He grins. "Too late. Show me how much you hate me. Let me *feel* that."

CHAPTER FOURTEEN

Lucifer reaches me. I stop retreating.

His hands are on my skin and my mind is lost.

I crash against him, sticking my tongue so far into his mouth that he grunts in surprise. I bite his bottom lip, hard. His blood hits my taste buds and my body explodes. I'm hit by a thousand volts of pure adrenalin, zinging with power.

"W-what is that?" I stutter.

"My blood?" He shrugs with a smirk. "*That*, my love, is something I never gift to anyone. Do you realize how fortunate you are?"

Yes, I do.

It's like crack. I need more.

I attack his mouth again, shoving him into a wall and sucking on his lip. He chuckles, fingers digging into my hips. "Slow down," he somehow mumbles with me still attached to his face. I don't heed his warning, so he forcefully removes me and holds me at arm's length.

"You can't have too much!" He chastises me like a greedy child.

"Why?" I pout.

He thinks on it. Raises his eyebrows. "I don't know. I've never done it. But I imagine you could overdose. It's potent—"

"Get over yourself." I kick his balls so that his grip on me loosens, then I'm on him again like a crazed addict. His kisses have blasted me into a new stratosphere. His blood tastes unlike anything else. I've sampled demon blood before, and it was fairly intoxicating, but it pales into insignificance compared to this. I'm vibrating with his wicked darkness surging through every nerve.

I drag myself away from his lips, long enough to search those fathomless eyes. I don't know what I'm looking for. It might be permission? I want to do things I've never done with him before. I want to take this power rushing through me and *use* it.

"Fine." He growls. "Take what you need. And don't say the Devil never shows mercy."

I don't give him a second to change his mind. Especially since he recently promised to only offer me punishments until I submitted. I hope he doesn't suddenly remember that.

Yanking down the remains of his jeans, I strip him bare and worship his body. Starting with that deep V cut at his hips, I lap at the splattered crimson droplets of the guard's blood. Lucifer moans in pleasure, letting me lick all the way along his abs, upward, finding a nipple and capturing it between my teeth.

"Such a wicked thing," he muses. "Lick me clean, Angel. Take all that blood and bathe in the power."

"I want more of yours, not theirs. Give me yours."

"Take it, then."

I assess his body. I don't have any knives on me. And his lip has already healed.

Terrifying, *thrilling* memories surface. The monster. The true Devil. The horns and *claws*.

"Give me the real Lucifer again. Turn back," I plead.

He frowns. "Angel—"

"Do it!" I yell, this frantic addiction crippling me. I *need* this.

He grips my chin firmly. "Such a demanding pet. I give an inch and you take a mile."

"Please."

"Louder."

"Please!" I scream, never more certain of anything in my life. I'm going to fuck a true monster and I'm dripping with the need for it. "Or are *you* nothing more than a useless *demon*?"

"Oh, clever girl." Eyes narrowing, his skin begins to glow. His wings expand. *Everything* expands. He's gigantic. At least two feet taller than usual. I crane my neck to look up into the face of Hell.

I step back, away, away, *away*... then I charge, hitting him in the guts, tackling him to the ground. I know he could have held firm. I'd have just bounced straight off his solid form. But he relents with a deep chuckle.

I straddle him victoriously, his mighty erection poking into my belly as I lean down. *Everything* grew bigger. Schlong included. There's *no way* this thing is going to fit inside me. It's no longer anywhere near the realms of even the most endowed human. He's always been generously endowed, but this is obscene.

Hesitantly, I run a finger over the head of his giant red shaft. It jerks at the touch and he shudders slightly.

"Scared?" he growls, watching me palm his length slowly up and down.

"Of you? Please!" I laugh, too high. "Get over—"

"Myself. Yes, you've said that before." He yanks my hair, dragging me down to his lips as he leans up to meet me. "Then stop stalling with gentle caresses to my cock and use it. And take note, I don't offer this without payment being expected, Angel. I did not forget my promise to you. This is yet another show of goodwill on my part. I'm letting you take control here. I have never—"

"Fuck's sake, shut up and bleed for me"—I grab the horns on his head, slamming it into the rock beneath us —"*my King*."

His eyes flare crimson bright.

Reaching into the minuscule space between us, he tips his head back and softly drags a black claw across his throat, splitting the flesh just enough that it doesn't gape in a gruesome mess. It's clean, almost delicate, but it bleeds. *Oh, how it bleeds.*

Licking and sucking, I take and take and take, until I'm flying so high that I barely hear when he snarls, "Enough." I keep going until he repeats himself and the wound magically heals. The flow stops, but it has leaked all over his chest, ebbing across taut skin and muscle.

Shimmying down, I assess his *member* with fresh eyes. Now, I'm so drunk on his essence, nothing can frighten me. It's long, thick, glowing deep red like the rest of him. I lick the tip then open wide, trying to take him into my throat. But despite my efforts, I can't accommodate more than a fraction of what's on offer.

Frustrated, I position my knees on either side of his hips and line up. Slowly, I begin the descent into madness. The width stretches me to my limits. Stinging and burning. I wriggle and grind, crying out.

"Perhaps I should return to a more normal si—"

"No!" I snap, cutting him off. I will not be defeated by a gigantic cock, even if it does belong to the King of Hell.

"Maybe some lubricant, then?" The Devil offers, watching me casually with pure amusement, simultaneously looking like a beast and a god. It's confusing. He looks more demonic in this form than ever before, and I know he could break me with a mere blink of his eyes, but he's playful, teasing, holding back the usual savage rush to either plunder or punish me.

He nods at his chest.

My pulse skitters at what he's suggesting. Then a sharp tang of arousal has me swiping my palms through the blood, collecting as much as I can before rubbing him down, coating him in slippery red essence.

I try again.

It's not as effective as *actual* lube, but it helps a little. Easing cautiously down his length, I'm already full and pained before he's even halfway inside. He growls and it rumbles through the walls. Shadows dance around us. "My patience grows thin."

Grabbing my hips, he holds me in place and thrusts upward, spearing me so deeply that I shriek at the top of my lungs.

"That's my good girl. Scream for me."

Oh, I scream all right.

Because just like that, the playful illusion shatters, and Lucifer is done letting me have control. I had so many ideas for how I would dominate *him* during this rare moment of giving, but his monster can't be caged any longer. He flips us around and pounds into me with that ridiculously oversized weapon until I'm certain that I'm tearing apart from the inside out.

But the power of his blood still courses through me, and although it's painful, it's also devastatingly delicious. I don't care if it kills me. He could literally tear me apart, and I'd still be begging for more.

With each scream, his mouth slants over mine in an open kiss, inhaling my pain and shuddering in pleasure. Tears track down my cheeks. He swiftly licks them away with a long, forked tongue. "The taste of your fear and pain is exquisite."

That tongue does unimaginable things to me.

Because surprisingly, Lucifer withdraws the painful rod from between my legs and replaces it with his mouth. He laps all around, carefully sampling every inch of bruised, torn skin. Then he's inside me, reaching depths that a tongue should never manage, swirling all around before darting in and out rapidly, thrusting until I'm screaming with pure *pleasure*.

I clutch his horns, pulling and urging him deeper still. Grinding my hips up and down, humping his face. His wings billow out in an ominous cloud of shadow and smoke.

Warmth pools in my belly, everything twitching in anticipation as the orgasm approaches. His tongue repeatedly switches from flicking gently over my electrified clitoris to plunging and plundering inside.

"Oh, God!" I yell.

He pauses the assault. "God can't help you. You might want to redirect your begging my way. I'll accept Lucifer or my King."

And with that, he sends me over the edge, licking me into a shivering mess, climax hitting hard.

"My turn." Without giving me a moment to catch my breath, he looms over me and slices a claw across my breast. There's a sharp sting followed by the press of lips as he sucks at my life force.

"I don't heal like you, asshole!" I bellow, feebly pushing his shoulders.

But I don't care.

Maybe I never did.

The rhythmic pull as he thrusts and sucks, sucks and thrusts, spirals me into further delirium.

"You wanted the beast. You've unleashed the hidden side of me now, Angel." His mighty voice once again shakes the very foundations of the building. I bet they can hear his words all the way back on Earth. "I'm going to take you this way every single day. I'm going to bleed for you. And you're going to bleed for me. We're going to murder and sacrifice and bathe in *their* blood. And you're going to beg for more and more."

I don't fight it.

He's right.

I'm never going to get enough of this sick love.

I claw at him like a hellcat. I bite him everywhere I can get close enough, teeth dragging on his skin, trying my hardest to hurt him. I punch and kick. I struggle and scream. All the while rocking my hips for more. And so he takes me, over every surface, from every angle, over and over until I pass out.

CHAPTER FIFTEEN

"Good morning," Lucifer speaks, bright and cheery, like he didn't activate savage beast mode last night—some bizarre mix of rabid hellish creature and earth-shatteringly stunning porn star.

I'm in his bed.

This only happened once before, early on... since then I've always been returned to my cell. Does he think I'm ready to give him what he wants now?

'I don't offer this without payment being expected, Angel.'

Maybe I am ready. Because, shit, I'm having zero luck in escaping from my current accommodations.

Wait. Have I even *tried* to escape?!

When was the last time I looked for routes, plotted, scanned for weapons?

"When will this end?" I groan, pressing my face into the pillow.

I'm lying on my side and he's behind me, pressed into my ass. *Fucking spooning!*

"I'm hoping you've felt enough wrath that maybe I can offer a little comfort again. We'll see how it goes."

Wrath.

The Devil is the master of inflicting pain. But I'm under no illusions here. I know that even the worst of the pain he's given me is no more than I can take. Purposefully laced with pleasure, keeping me on the edge. Balancing. Ready to topple into his snare and never come out.

But damn, if he doesn't love to receive it, too.

Show me how much you hate me.

It didn't matter how hard I bit him, how hard I tore him apart with nails and fists. He was always ready for more. I don't need to look to know that his torso will now be as perfectly sculpted and unblemished as usual. No bite marks. Nothing to show just how much I *hated* him last night.

Mine, though? The cuts and bruises shine through. Trophies to remind me how sick I am. My back stings as phantom lashes pass across it. Between my legs feels *brutalized*.

Is that what he does to the tortured souls he claims? Over and over... but without any of the pleasure tacked on?

"Doesn't the devil reap the *souls* of those sold to him? Shouldn't I be dead? Yanked from my mortal body?" Realization makes my heart skip.

"How do you know you're not?" His hand rests on my hip, searing my skin from the heat of his gentle touch. I feel him bone-deep, *everywhere*.

My mouth hangs open.

"Relax, I'm kidding. *Living* human toys are much more fun to play with… until they break, anyway."

Yeah, that's not comforting.

"How does that even work? If you're dead and here as a soul, are you still in a human form? How else would you feel pain? How would you be punished?"

"Let's hope you have a few years left before you break and find out."

My throat closes up. My eyes go wide.

I twist my neck to look at him and find him biting his lip, failing to hide a smile. I grab my pillow and whack it against his head. He chuckles, flinging it away.

It's not funny. *Quit grinning with him, Angel!*

"Come on, I want to know. The infernal dungeon. What's it really like?"

His smile turns thoughtful, ghosting his lips, a serene faraway look in his eyes. "*Stunning.*"

"You're one sick puppy." I push up to my knees and lob another pillow at him.

"As are you, my Angel." His head tips to the side as he grins at me. I hate the way he does that. *The cocked head, the playful look, the beautiful face…*

"Your demons think you'll send them down just for talking about it."

"They're not wrong. If they're that curious, they deserve a demonstration."

"*I'm* curious," I prod for some unknown reason other than I'm an idiot.

"You're different."

"Why?"

He doesn't answer. He doesn't need to.

We both know he adores me because I'm somehow cut from the same rotten cloth as him.

I've been called a sadist before. I prefer to think of myself as a connoisseur of pain. It's an art form. There are so many varying shades, so many ways to paint the canvas of suffering.

He sits up, coming in behind me again, and runs a finger gently along an old, half-healed whip mark on my back. I jolt against his touch.

"This"—his finger presses harder against the mark—"was a mistake." His voice is low, hoarse. "I'm sorry."

He just apologized to me.

I can't compute.

His breath hitches as his fingers pass from one welt to another. "I should never have hurt you like that. You're not like everyone else. You have to be different. *I* have to be different. I'm still learning, but I don't want to be the same with you. I don't want to hurt you."

"I like you hurting me." My whole body quivers. His words are confusing, and my body doesn't agree with anything my head says.

"You didn't like these." Fingers whisper over the lashings. "I went too far that night. I won't ever go beyond your limits again."

This is beyond my limits.

I can't sit here having this conversation. Talking like we're a couple setting up safe words for our kinky times, like it's all fun and loving and normal.

There's nothing remotely fucking normal about any of this. And his apologies don't mean shit.

Especially since I wasn't even mad at him, anyway.

I should be mad at him!

My gaze lands on a door in the nearest wall. More like a hatch, really. It's too small for a person to fit through and positioned halfway up the wall.

"Go ahead. Open it if you really want to, but I'd advise you don't." Lucifer's hands fall from my back. He knows full well that telling me not to do something is going to have me running for it.

I approach it with caution. Barely noticing the fact I'm naked. When did I last wear clothes, besides skimpy underwear? How long have I been here?

Slowly, I pull the latch and swing the door. The room floods with deafening screams. Bellowing. Wailing. Groaning.

The sound is so intense that my head spins. It echoes around the room, bouncing from wall to wall and seeming to amplify as it goes.

I slam the door shut and fall back against it breathlessly. "What in the ever-loving fuck?"

The Devil shrugs, looking way too amused. "It's my entertainment system. The sound carries directly from the infernal dungeon via a series of chutes."

Okay, his level of sickness is way beyond my boundaries.

"Most people just get a TV!" I gasp. "Maybe a games console!"

Letting myself believe I know this man is a

dangerous game. I could never understand him in a million years.

Oh, but you do understand. Too well, my inner voice taunts. For once it really is my own conscience and not his ragged timbre in my head.

You bathe in their blood. He listens to their screams. Really, what's the difference?

I feel my face pale. "Holy shit, do you jerk off to that noise?"

He shakes his head in mock disapproval. "Angel, my castle is full of whores waiting to please me. I don't need to *jerk off*. But anyway, no, I don't use the infernal screams to get me off." He pauses, running those black eyes up and down my body. "I use the screams of the whores themselves."

Bull's-eye.

His words feel like a red-hot poker through my guts. "And do they? Please you?" I ask before I can stop myself.

His smile fades. "No, they do not."

"I'm not a whore."

"I've never suggested so."

"Nor are they. They're *women*. Held here and forced into your harem against their will."

He shrugs. Then closes the distance between us. Takes my hands. Rests his forehead against mine. "I've never been with anyone who meant anything before."

"Me neither."

I feel his smile against my neck as he buries himself into me.

"That's not what I meant." I shove him away. "All I

meant is that I've never cared for anyone before. I wasn't suggesting that you're different." I stumble over my words, retreating to a safe distance.

He huffs a long-suffering sigh and pours a whiskey. Hands me the glass. I've had nothing but drops of water since my arrival. I down it instantly.

Do what he wants.

Let him get you drunk and say the words he wants to hear.

End this.

I take the bottle from him and chug until my throat burns.

CHAPTER
SIXTEEN

I'M STARTING TO QUITE LIKE MY CELL.

At least, that's what I tell myself when I'm thrown back into it after once again ending the day by telling Lucifer to *go fuck himself*.

Another few weeks have passed as far as I can tell.

It's been a little different these weeks. He never hurts me more than I beg for. Yet still, I fight him. I'm such a confused mess. I plead for his cock one moment and then try to slice it off the next.

But no matter how hard I try to kill him during our sexy time—all lust and violence mixed into bloody carnage—I always awake in his bed now. Relaxed. At peace. *Content*.

And he's always a different man in those moments. Like a *real* man. Open, honest, humorous. Calm. His black eyes more of a slate gray.

We laugh. Talk. *Breathe*.

I drink copious amounts of alcohol to numb what's coming.

Because then he makes his offer. The same, every day.

Freedom, in exchange for different chains—invisible ones. *Pledge myself to him.*

No matter how I bite my tongue until it bleeds, despite myself, in opposition to what I want to do—I tell him to go fuck himself.

Evidently, I make a great submissive in the bedroom, but a truly appalling one out of it.

But maybe I'm making some progress. Sure, I'm back in my cell. Today, though, he hasn't had me chained up. I'm free to sit on the stone floor. Such *luxury*.

Seriously, though, I *do* kinda like it. It's just me. I don't have to interact with anyone. I don't have to worry about when I'm going to get my next fix, about how many demons I'll have to kill this time for peace to briefly soothe me again.

Because that's something that has taken longer and longer with each passing year; it's harder to settle the violent energy inside me. Here, it's all taken away. I don't have to think about anything. I just exist, from one moment to the next, nothing to worry about other than when my next orgasm will arrive. Or whipping. Who's monitoring?

Holy shit. I need to get out of this place.

Is this Stockholm syndrome? Sitting here *looking forward* to my next visit from the Devil! What kind of magic does he possess to have me feeling like this?

"There's no magic. It's all you, you sick bitch," I mutter aloud to myself.

A deep shadow creeps along the corridor and fills the doorway.

I snort. "Speak of the Devil and he really does appear!"

Lucifer materializes amidst the swirling shadows, onyx-feathered wings lazily adjusting behind him. "Ever one to please." He smirks, and the door swings open. He holds out a hand to me.

I regard him with skepticism.

"Come!" His head jerks in an upward motion.

"Where?" I cautiously step through the doorway, knocking his outstretched hand aside.

"To play outside the castle."

"You're taking me on a date?" My jaw unhinges in mock horror at my joke.

He shrugs. "All the sex, blood, and lashings haven't quite done the job yet. Maybe you need a little more from me? A little romance?"

I guffaw, slapping a hand over my mouth at the pig noise that escaped. He frowns, then turns around and begins walking.

"Seriously, where are we going?"

"We don't have movie theaters in Hell," he calls over his shoulder as I trail after him. "Or restaurants. So, I'm taking you for some live action."

"A theater?"

"Of sorts. More like a gladiatorial stage."

Bewildered, I follow him through long, lonely

passageways until we reach a huge arched door. It swings open with a flick of his wrist. The sentries standing on either side bow their heads, eyes to the floor.

Lucifer turns to face me, casting his wicked gaze up and down my mostly naked form.

This sonofabitch is actually serious. "I can't go anywhere dressed like this!"

I've become accustomed to the lingerie, but let's face it, my time here has just been one long sex-fest. I can't go outside in underwear!

"You look perfect." He grins.

My feet root to the ground. I raise my brows. If he pushes me on this, I'm going to kick his ass in front of his guards.

Sensing the disobedience that's about to flood out of me, he tips his head back and sighs. His wings billow and flap in a smoky haze.

Shadows creep toward me. I step back, holding out a defensive hand, but the motion is useless. They wrap around me. I tense, waiting to feel choked and constrained, but the shifting blackness settles into something resembling a cape. It flows from my shoulders right to my feet. My torso is mostly covered from the front, though my legs are still on display. I try to touch it, but despite the solid-ish appearance, my fingers feel nothing. Still, it does the job, concealing me within his shimmering umbra.

"Satisfied?" he asks.

"Not really. Flashy bastard." I skulk past him, immediately getting hit in the face by the thick, oppressive air outside the castle. Red, sunless sky hangs over nothing but black rock. Dark buildings rise up ahead.

He walks and I fall in step beside him.

"Care to hold hands?" His face flickers with amusement.

"What do you think?"

"Your loss."

We don't speak again. The farther we walk, the more his playfulness vanishes, replaced with stern authority. Every demon we pass drops to their knees in his presence. Guards avert their eyes respectfully, but the normal demons going about their business bend the knee. He seems to grow taller, more imposing, as his shadows grow deeper with every step we take.

They tighten protectively around me. I've spent my life fearing his shadows. Now I'm literally cloaked inside them and it's... comforting. Enveloped in his dark, thrumming energy, my pulse races and then settles into something that feels strangely like contentment.

We enter a city, of sorts, and the small crowds part for us. They all have a look of complete shock on their faces before they regain their wits and drop into sickening subservience. My guess is that Lucifer doesn't take many outings.

I try to remain indifferent, but I can't help it; before long I feel like I'm walking a little taller too, chin held high, enjoying the malice emanating beside me and the fact that I'm *with* him.

The crowds thicken. There's so much shouting and shoving that many now fail to notice who's amongst them. He doesn't seem to mind. He simply continues his path, leading me through the masses, past security guards, and into an amphitheater hewn from the obsidian hell-rock.

The noise is deafening. Demons worked into a frenzy, screaming at those in the ring who are beating the ever-loving shit out of each other. Vast arrays of weapons line the arena. Blood coats the floor. There are bodies piled up in one corner.

"My King!" A demon dressed in a suit appears in front of us, nervously wringing his hands. "We weren't expecting you. We don't have—"

Lucifer flaps a hand dismissively. "I don't require anything today."

Confused, the demon attempts to say something else, but Lucifer snaps his fingers, and the man disappears into a poof of black smoke.

"Was that necessary?!" I gasp.

"Yes. Sniveling kiss-asses are tedious, and you know it."

Can't argue with that, I suppose.

Surprise jolts me as we step from the raucous crowds into an area completely isolated. A vast rocky platform with two thrones at the top and not a single other soul. The space feels wonderful. It's already hard to breathe in Hell's heated air, without masses of bodies adding to the claustrophobia.

Lucifer settles himself into the largest throne. I go to sit next to him, but he grabs my wrist.

"My love, I've given you plenty of chances, but you haven't quite earned that seat yet, have you?" One eyebrow goes up in confrontation.

"You sat me next to you once, the time you had me kill that demon. Why—"

"That wasn't a throne. It was a simple chair." He pats the ornately carved seat beside him. "*This* is a throne, and you know what you need to do for it."

"Fine, I'll stand," I grit.

But he still has hold of my wrist, and he yanks me into his lap. "Like hell you will." His deep rumble vibrates through me. Squirming is useless as both arms wrap around my waist, pinning me against him.

Fuck this shit.

I'm sitting in his lap.

And it feels *way* too good.

My body vibrates with nervous excitement. His grip tightens as he presses his face into my neck, deliberately inhaling deeply. Goose bumps erupt all over me.

"Don't let me distract you from the show." One hand reaches down, absently running along my thigh.

I clamp my legs together and do as instructed, zeroing my focus on the bloody battlefield where there are currently three hellhounds snarling at a solitary man as he wildly swings an axe around.

From the corner of my eye, another suited demon loiters, watching us, stepping forward, then back. Eventually, he takes a deep breath and marches over. "My King, apologies for the interruption, but—"

"Not interested," Lucifer snarls, fingers now gripping my thigh painfully.

"But it's important. There's news that Lil—"

"*Not* now!" he bellows so loudly that the ground rumbles and the stadium falls silent, all heads turning our way. I twist to face him as he pinches the bridge of his nose. Then his fingers come together like he's about to click them.

"No!" I swipe at his hand. "Don't smoke him for doing his job!"

Wait, why am I protecting a demon? What do I care!

I press my lips together against any further protest, but it seems I've already saved this jerk's ass.

"Later," Lucifer growls. "She can wait. Find me later."

The demon nods and hurries away.

Gradually, the noise levels resume, and attention returns to the bloody action.

Lucifer is solid marble beneath me, every muscle tense with angry energy. I don't know what that was about. But he said *she* and a weird jealousy zaps my nerves. What other woman is so important that the demon would demand an audience? And what woman would make Lucifer react this way?

I bristle just as much as the Devil. Any former feelings of fun on our little *date* have dissipated. All I feel is cold and uneasy.

I try to focus back on the show. After all, fighting is

one of my favorite things. But it's not long before Lucifer mercifully gives up on this whole charade.

"This was a mistake. I should attend to business." He stands, dumping me unceremoniously from his lap.

Business with another woman.

Ice settles in my core as we head back to the castle.

CHAPTER
SEVENTEEN

AFTER A NIGHT OF FESTERING IN CONFUSING JEALOUSY, JENNA arrives at my cell with my soup, looking more nervous than usual. I mean, she's always edgy, but today there's an extra skittishness about her. Casting manic glances up and down the corridor, she unlocks the cell door and swings it wide.

I stand there staring, waiting to be informed of what *Master* wants this time. Am I to bathe in rose petals prior to having the skin flayed from my back?

No. *Because he's no longer hurting me beyond my limits...*

Perhaps another weird date then before ditching me for another woman?

My teeth grind.

Lucifer never spoke another word last night. Just ripped his shadow cloak away and dumped me back in my cell. He was fuming about something. Skin glowing red, the true beast threatening to emerge. I matched his rage, blood boiling at my own stupidity.

"Now's your chance." Jenna yanks my seraph blade from beneath her flowing skirt and thrusts it at me. For a moment, I think she's trying to stab me, and I dodge, ready to strike back. But she just gawks at me in despair, hurriedly thrusting it forward again. "Master is away, dealing with Lilith's mess."

Lilith.

The other woman.

That's the name that had been on the demon's tongue before he silenced him.

So, another woman really was more important than finishing our evening.

Cocking my head, I take a tentative step toward her, worried she'll either bolt or swipe at me. She could do either, judging by her trembling hands. As soon as I take the blade, she reaches into her corset and pulls out a map.

"This will lead you out of the castle. And here"—she flips the paper over and points at a circled spot—"this side is a map for beyond the castle. You'll find a permanent hellgate at the circle. It's heavily guarded."

"Why are you doing this?"

"You could have let the guards punish me, and you could have let Master punish me. You didn't have to perform for him just to save me. I must repay the debt."

My eyes narrow. "You could just say thanks."

She lets out a sharp sigh.

"Or maybe I should thank you," I offer. "You stepped up so I wouldn't have to choose a strange woman. You not only made the whole thing bearable, but dare I say it, *enjoyable.*" I smirk.

She shakes her head, brushing it off. "My time here runs short. I've served the required years. Master will soon send me down for my sins. I can't escape the inferno forever, unless maybe... if you were to *remove* him."

There's no way this little mouse has done anything in her life to deserve the inferno!

"I'm not what you think!" she shrieks. "I did bad things. He'll make me suffer. *More...*" Without elaborating further, she retreats, smoothing her skirt and taking a steadying breath. "Please. You're my only hope. If you destroy him, it might set me free."

Destroy him.

My traitorous heart lurches at the idea, bringing bile to my throat. I'm going to have to do something about that when the time comes.

"Hurry," she barks, spurring me to life.

"How do you know he won't return any second?" I look around, instinctively seeking out the supplies that I always grab before a mission. But all I have is the knife and the map.

Just *one knife* to aid my escape from Hell.

"He's far away. He won't return for at least another day."

"Forgive my bluntness, but Lucifer doesn't seem like the type to discuss his whereabouts with his slaves." I step from the cell, swinging my gaze along the dark corridor. I hear the heavy footfall of guards passing nearby. I hope it is just guards and not hellhounds.

Jenna flinches at my words. "No, he doesn't. But one of his generals is very sweet on *this* slave and all too eager to spill secrets when my lips are around his dick. He doesn't see me as anything but a toy. No brain. No drive. No mind of my own. He told me they'll be gone for days."

I've underestimated this woman.

"Who is Lilith?" I ask, bringing another knot to my throat.

"No time," she snaps.

"Fine. At least tell me who *you* are, really, Jenna."

She smiles for the first time *ever*. "I'm no one. But with your success, maybe I'll be one of the instigators in ending his reign."

⬢

I DUCK AND WEAVE THROUGH ENDLESS CORRIDORS LIKE SOME sort of stealth-pro-ninja. Only, I'm wearing a damned corset and little else. And the weaving might be because I'm drunk.

Okay, my ninja skills are a little off form.

But the seraph blade hums in my grip, purring with delight at our reunion and at the sheer number of demons around us. I know it *feels* them because I can feel its excitement.

Or maybe it's just my own thrill and I'm blaming it on a blade rather than examining my own sick desires.

Regardless. The blade sings. My stomach coils in

anticipation. And I pass through the castle like an invisible wraith, only stumbling once or twice. Any demons I encounter are so shocked to see me on the loose, it barely takes any effort to slit their throats.

At first, I try to drag the bodies into doorways, hide them... but it takes too long. I need to get out of here *fast*. So I leave a bloody trail in my wake, running, pace increasing with each new corridor, waiting for the alarm to go off within the castle walls.

Rounding a corner, I charge right into three more demons. Not guards, just ordinary demons, visiting... what *do* they do here? Do they come for the entertainment? Do they hope to gain favor from Lucifer by hanging around, waiting for the right moment to impress him?

One of them grabs my throat.

I slam the blade into his temple. He falls away, blackness escaping in a steady stream. It's funny—on Earth, the smoky soul always floats upward and away. Here, it sinks straight down through the stone floor. Right into the abyss.

The other two make a grab for me. Why don't they run?! Is my outfit too disorienting? Maybe it should become my new uniform. *How to fool a demon in one outfit choice—*

The biggest of the pair yanks my hair. "Sweet Jesus, are you *trying* to arouse me with this foreplay?" Ducking and ramming my elbow into his guts, I spin free and take one lightning swipe at him, followed by another to his female friend.

They drop.

I resume running.

There are loud noises from the floor above. Shouting. Heavy footfall.

Shit. They've found the first bodies.

It's hard to read a map while running. Especially when it all looks the same. A million turnings and identical corridors. What's inside all these rooms, anyway? I wish I had time to look. But I'm realizing my map-reading skills are as lacking as my present stealth skills. And I might be going around in circles.

My foot catches on something heavy as I'm looking at the map and I go flying, landing with such force that the skin shreds from my knees and the air whooshes from my lungs.

"Motherfucking fuck!" I find my feet and deliver a swift kick to the dead demon body on the ground. One I already killed ten minutes ago.

Yeah. I seriously suck at escaping.

But then I turn the map, look at it from a fresh angle, and see that the exit isn't off a corridor at all. It's *up*.

Looking above me, I keep my eyes to the ceiling as I run. Until, just as the sound of angry demons advancing on me is starting to make me question this plan, I see it —the markings carved into the stone overhead.

Standing beneath them, I wait.

I growl impatiently.

I study the map once more and find tiny words scrawled along the edge.

Claws scrape on stone. A deep growl makes my

stomach lurch to my throat. Three hellhounds stalk toward me. Hideous lips curled back, drool dripping from teeth...

"*Dimettere est anima mea*," I breathe.

With a sickening sliding sensation, the walls shift around me, the floor seems to disappear, the hellhounds lunge... and then I'm outside in the sweltering heat beyond the castle walls.

That was too close.

Thanks for the heads-up on *looking up*, Jenna. What else haven't you told me?!

I study my new surroundings, trying to make sense of where I am. Why doesn't the map have one of those '*You Are Here*' arrows? But it does show the castle, which I can see behind me, and this narrows down my location. There are no buildings ahead like there was when I stepped out with Lucifer. I must have come out the back way.

Come on, Angel, this map is far simpler than the one inside.

There just aren't many landmarks to go by in aligning myself. There are mountains in the distance, there's black rock, and more black rock, and more... in a sweeping plateau as far as the eye can see. Above me, the sunless red sky presses down, sweltering heat smothering me like a bag over my head.

That lingering sound of distant screams feels like it's all around. Everywhere and nowhere. You can't hear it inside the castle. Unless you open Lucifer's *entertainment* hatch.

Trusting instinct, I set off in another sprint, rapidly running out of breath.

What if this hellgate is invisible too? Like the escape through the ceiling. What if I run right past it? It makes sense it would be hidden; he's not just going to have a gate with a welcome sign, is he?

Stumbling past a huge outcrop of the black lava-veined rock, I draw to a skidding stop, quickly dragging myself back behind the rock face and peeking out.

There, in full blazing sight, is a glowing purple portal. Protected by at least ten guards. With a line of demons waiting to pass through.

A fucking *line?!*

They're queuing up in this orderly fashion, waiting their turn, getting called forward for some sort of identification scan before passing through and disappearing. It's ridiculously civilized.

I'm paralyzed. Frozen in wonder and utter confusion. Slightly drunk befuddlement.

The portal shimmers, warping the air around it. I'm suddenly a little scared at what could happen when I touch it. As far as I know, higher level demons can materialize in and out of Hell at will, dragging humans with them. But without a demon pilot, for want of a better word, this is the only way out.

Gripping the rock beside me for support, my legs start to waver. It feels like an eternity since Jenna opened my cage and I've spent the whole time just waiting to get caught. I'm used to danger, used to fighting or running, depending on the situation—but this is new.

This is some crazy mix of being terrified of getting caught and *wanting* to get caught.

Because, seriously, what happens when I get back home? Is the Devil just going to say, '*Oh well, she escaped. Never mind.*'

Hell no. He's going to be right back on my ass and there isn't a single ward or protection spell that can hide me from him.

Not when my soul is literally calling out to him, craving him—

A sharp pain draws my attention to my hand, gripping the rock so hard that a jagged section has sliced into my palm.

"Okay. Focus. You can do this." Straightening up, I look down once again at my corset. I'm actually going to march up to a hellgate to kill a whole herd of demons, wearing *this* shit. My life has fallen to new lows.

The way I see it, there are two options now.

I hang back and wait for this absurdly organized line of demons to pass through, then take on the guards. Or I make a mad suicidal dash for it, past them all, and pray that leaping headfirst into a hellgate is enough to get you through to the other side, that you don't need anything special—

Someone grips my elbow, yanking me out from my hiding place. My blade is still clutched in my other hand, which I slash upward toward my captor. It's swiftly knocked from my grip and kicked away in contempt.

My gaze swings up from the stilettos and long legs,

over the figure-hugging little black dress, and into a pair of impatient demon eyes.

"You're with me. Just keep looking at your feet, don't make eye contact, and for the love of Satan, *say nothing*."

Pulling firmly on my elbow, she walks us slowly toward the line.

My mouth flaps open and closed uselessly. Since speech isn't coming, I dig my heels in. She spins to face me, anger flaring across her delicate face. All porcelain skin and long black hair, beautiful in a haunting, creepy way.

"Walk. Now," she growls in my ear. "You're going to draw attention to us."

My feet mirror hers, as if they have a will of their own, because I certainly do not trust this bitch as we join the back of the line. I have no clue wh—

"Quit staring at me like you want to kill me and keep your gaze on the floor, *Angel*. Or do you want those guards to become suspicious? I'd hoped for more intelligence from you," she whispers.

"Who the fuck are you?" Self-preservation kicks in and I stare at my feet. Then back at hers. How the hell did she walk over these rocks in heels like that? She looks like she's practically floating, all grace and poise. And that dress! Barely covering her ass. Ugh. Demons are so *extra*.

"I'm L... yra."

"Lllll... yra?" I taunt, glancing up briefly into her annoyed eyes. Tell me this isn't *her*. No, it can't be. Jenna said he was *away* with Lilith.

"Yes, Lyra. And I'm your *only* shot out of here, so I suggest you show some gratitude."

"You're a demon. A bullshitting one."

"Is there any other sort?"

"What's in this for you?"

"I've had enough of Lucifer's hypocritical tyranny. I saw you at the castle and had Jenna free you. Us sisters have to stick together, right?"

I snort.

She snorts back.

I just shared a joke with a demon.

And the Devil is under my skin, calling out to me—

We step closer to the gate, waiting patiently like everyone else. There's constant chatter around us. No one pays us any attention. They're all just talking and laughing and waiting. It's so damn *normal.*

"Do all hellgates have security checks like this?" I slur, hating Lucifer for giving me whiskey on this day of all days.

"Only those close to the King's castle."

"Can't you just snap your fingers and *poof* us out of here?" My feet continue to drag as we inch closer to the portal.

"Again, not close to the castle. It allows him to monitor who's close to him."

I can't help it, my feet have rooted to the ground again. The swirling portal looks like it'll surely hurt, rip me apart.

"Look," Lyra continues, whispering into my ear just in case of eavesdroppers, "let's just say I'm on the opposing team to Lucifer and if his reign topples, I won't be crying. And keep moving, you coward, it won't hurt."

"And how exact—"

"Sshh." Her grip tightens on my elbow, and she marches me to the guards.

This was a mistake. She's going to hand me over and get some sort of reward. I just stood here and let her lead me right to them.

"Name?" the closest guard asks her while staring at me. I drop my gaze.

"Lyra. I'm returning this one topside. I have a game I want to play with her."

"Oh yeah? What's that?" The guard steps into my space. I have the overwhelming urge to stare back defiantly, but for once in my life, I do as I'm told. Lyra pulls me closer to her side.

"Oh, you know, just a little hunting. She's a good runner. Pretty good fighter, too. I have a group of paying customers waiting to chase her down. In fact, we're already late, so if you don't mind."

"And what if *I* want to buy her?" The guard grips my chin, forcing me to look at him.

There's only so much I can do. I can force my eyes down, I can act meek, but once our eyes meet, I can't stop the defiance that sparks in them, the threatening glare I offer him. If he doesn't let go of me in three seconds—

"I'll find you another," Lyra croons, running a finger over his collarbone. "But this one has been purchased by one of the seven. And you know how cranky Lucifer gets if they give him shit." She offers him a smile, and he rolls his eyes in return.

"Fine, but make sure you come back if you get more like her. I can feel it in her energy. She's a real livewire."

"Sure thing, babe."

He lets go of me, after one last lingering gawk at my tits, and Lyra presses me toward the glowing purple gate.

"Close the gate!" A deep voice bellows from behind us. "Close that gate, right now!"

There's more yelling. I turn to see an army of demons descending on us. The security guard growls, lunging at Lyra.

"Shit." She sighs. "I'm so overdressed for this."

Her left hand goes into the air and the guard freezes mid-attack. His eyes bulge. Another horde leaps for us. That's the best word to describe the sheer number of demons all attacking us at once. This is it, the end—

They all freeze.

The whole of Hell for all I know. Certainly, everyone in our vicinity. They're all glued in position, motion stilled, angry voices lost to nothing. I could hear a pin drop.

The strain begins to show on Lyra's face as she holds it all. Veins pulse in her temples. She looks so unimposing in her heels and dress, her blindingly white skin, her serene posture. Then she screams and they all explode.

Blood and gore erupt in plumes and arcs, and amidst all this human gloop, a black fog swirls furiously. It whips over us, sending cascades of her dark hair billowing out around her. There's a horrible screaming, whistling noise. And then, *nothing*.

The smoky souls disappear, down into the abyss beneath us.

Flicking a lump of bone matter from her arm, Lyra graciously swings around to the hellgate. "Shall we?"

We step through.

⊛

It's like falling.

And flying.

Drowning. And soaring. And sinking.

That feeling in your belly when you drive over a hump too fast.

And then we're spat out into a darkness I haven't felt in forever. True, earthly darkness. With stars overhead and the glow of the city. Not like Hell where there's a perpetual red sky without a sun, or the gloom of his castle.

I'm *free*.

I'm out of Hell.

For how long? Run, my little Angel. Run, run, run...

I whirl around, trying to find him in the shadows. Find him *being* the shadows... but he's not physically here. *Yet*.

The enormity of this whole clusterfuck slams home. How does one hide from the Devil? When he supposedly owns you because of a deal?

He's already back inside my head.

"Who are you?" I shove Lyra's chest, forcing her to step back in shock.

"Lyra."

With a sigh, I yank the corset higher over my boobs and glance down at my bloody, grazed knees. A spray of something gloopy has smudged down my thigh. Getting back into civilization is going to suck looking like this. "An ordinary demon does not have that much power. Or the inclination to draw that much attention to themselves just to release a human from Hell."

"I never said I was an *ordinary* demon. You only asked my name."

Damned demons and their games.

"*What* are you?"

Her grin widens. "Well, that would be telling, and where's the fun in that? Discovery is so much more satisfying. I'm sure a hunter like yourself has a wealth of detective skills in their arsenal."

The hellgate can't be seen on this side, not without the right spells and exact location. My gaze darts anxiously, wondering when the first of Lucifer's demon legion is going to arrive to drag me back to Hell. Or will he come himself?

Something wholly inappropriate washes through me at the thought of his anger, his punishments—

"What do you want from me?" I return my attention to Lyra, who's muttering to herself about the blood on her stilettos.

She suddenly straightens up, giving me a hard, interested stare, as if I finally asked the right question. "You're the first human I've ever met to get under his skin. And we have a mutual desire to see Lucifer fall. You could have a decent shot in aiding the war."

"The war?"

"The war against the Devil has been raging for centuries."

An unbidden memory surfaces, of the way Lucifer slumped against the wall in my cage, looking entirely too human and vulnerable.

'Bad day at the office?'

'No more than usual.'

"He will destroy you, Angel." Lyra slips gracefully into my space, unassuming and threatening all at the same time. "We must destroy him first."

"We?"

"Play your part, and I'll see to it that you're rewarded."

My laughter hits her right in the face, causing her brows to pinch in disgust.

"Look, can you get me a weapon powerful enough to take him down? That's all I need, and I'll deal with this myself, without your *rewards*."

Now it's her turn to laugh. "Funny little human! I wasn't implying *you're* strong enough to kill him. Leave that to us big girls. All I'm saying is that you're under his skin and having him chase you around while you're running amok back on Earth is a perfectly timed distraction for us. That's it. That's your part. *Keep him busy.*"

Violence brews in my guts.

I might want to kill him, but I do not like hearing this bitch talking about doing it. He's *mine*.

She offers me an exaggerated sigh. "I see that look in your eyes and taking a shot at me will not end well for you, Angel. You don't even have your blade. What are you going to do?" Her hands go to her hips.

My own hands pat down my body. I growl in frustration. I *love* that blade—we were only just reunited and now it's discarded amongst the rocks in Hell. *Fuck this shit.*

"Well, I'd love to stay and bond further, but time is ticking." Lyra turns to leave. "Summon the demon Malphas. Tell him *the night is new and the raven has landed*. He'll hook you up with a ward strong enough to hide you from Lucifer. But going by previous experience, it won't last long. A week, maybe two. Make the most of it."

The retort is on my lips. The witty comeback about demons using lame, cryptic communication codes like they're in some eighties spy movie...

But she's vanished.

Chapter
Eighteen

He's been stalking me my whole life.

If I think I'm going to be able to hide from him, I'm an idiot.

But I don't need to hide from him. At least, not for long. I just need to get myself a suitable weapon and then I'll welcome him back.

With open *armed* arms.

After an excruciating journey across the city dressed like a brazen hooker, I retrieve my bag from my warehouse and pull on real clothes again. Then I make my way to Brooke's Salty Haven. He'll know to look for me here. I'd better be quick.

She lunges for me the moment our eyes meet across the bar. "Angel! Dammit, bitch, you better have a good excuse for not showing to your birthday party!" Brooke pulls me to a booth.

"I'm sorry. It wasn't my usual skipping town. There was shit that went down."

"What kind of shit?"

"I need a seraph dealer, but not the usual," I speak, voice low.

"Sure, I can hook you up with Tommy, or Killian, or that dude from Canada, what's his name? Pete? Paul? P—"

"You're not listening. I said *not* the usual. I need someone way above their pay grade. I'm talking highly specialized angel weapons. Shit, I probably need an *actual* angel."

Brooke leans forward. "What are we talking about here?"

I release a breath. "Let's say, hypothetically, that I need a blade to kill Lucifer."

"*Lucifer!*"

I nod, rolling my eyes at her lack of subtlety as half the bar glances our way.

"The Devil?" She leans into my space, talking in a manic half-whisper, nowhere near quiet enough.

"No, the fucking Christmas Elf!" I hiss.

She lets out a long whistle as she leans back. "Girl, what kind of messed-up shit are you keeping all to yourself this time? When you gonna start becoming a team player? Let us help."

"You are helping if you keep your mouth shut about this and just point me in the right direction of a blade."

She pouts.

I refuse to take the bait by engaging her in this. The less she knows, the better.

"Time is kind of ticking here," I finally mutter.

"All right, hold your panties, I'm thinking! You're going to want protection while you're organizing this. Keep you off the radar. You start even talking about this shit and he finds out—"

"Lyra's already fixed me up with a powerful ward. I just need a blade."

"Who's Lyra?"

"The demon who helped me escape Hell."

"You're trusting a *demon*!" Her hands land with a thump on the table.

"No, she's a liar! Well, maybe, a little."

"Angel!"

"Look, it's under control, okay?"

"Wait, you were in Hell?"

"Yeah, and knowing who to trust isn't so simple anymore. A trip to the dark side changes things. My *situation* changes things."

"And what exactly *is* this situation?"

I open my mouth to spill the whole story but sink back into my chair, swallowing the words. *Old habits die hard.*

Brooke shakes her head, black curls bouncing in agitation. But she doesn't push me further. She's learned how stubborn I am.

Drawing a phone from her pocket, she sends me a contact. "This dude ain't for messin' with. I hope you know what you're doing, Angel."

CHAPTER
NINETEEN

SUMMONING DEMONS IS SURPRISINGLY EASY. THEY LOVE THE opportunity to come along and screw with whichever poor, deluded sap thought that attracting demon attention was a good idea. Because nine times out of ten, the demon comes out on top.

We're talking schoolkids messing around, desperate people looking for some sort of trade to make their shitty life better, or amateur hunters getting too big for their boots.

Guys looking to trade their unborn kids' lives for the chance at a cheerleader orgy...

But anyway, even if the demon doesn't want to come, like when he knows there's a bitch called Angel waiting for him, it's not too hard to drag them here. You just need the right spells, equipment, expertise... and balls.

Malphas, though? This is some top-level demon shit that has my heart thrashing against my ribs. One wrong move, word... I'm toast.

I'm pretty sure he's one of the seven Princes of Hell. I haven't had time for much research, but some texts list him as second-in-command in Hell, with forty legions under his command. I never saw him when I was there. At least, not that I'm aware of. But if he really is that high up the chain, is he really going to come here and betray Lucifer like Lyra-the-Liar-who's-probably-Lilith says? If he is, then what does this say about Lucifer's hold over his kingdom? Is it really going to topple under the influence of backstabbers and war?

Not if I get there first...

The texts also list Malphas for his habit of accepting sacrifices offered to him, then deceiving the conjurer.

Exactly what sort of sacrifice is he going to ask of me?

I wipe clammy palms on my jeans after completing a salt circle in the middle of the room.

Asmodeus is also a Prince of Hell, but I was never scared summoning him. Not like this. Not this churning stomach, pushing bile into my throat. This isn't like me at all.

Because I'm not entirely sure *what* I'm afraid of. I've dealt with powerful demons before, but today something buzzes under my skin and dread pools in my guts. And I think it might not be anything to do with my mortality, with the sacrifice and deception that awaits, but instead, it might be to do with losing the Devil.

With actually carrying out this plan to end him.

As if on cue, a shadow streaks across the room on the edge of my vision. I spin around but can't see him anywhere. Has he found me already? Is this all for nothing? Jenna assured me he'd be busy for longer.

Without wasting any further time, I hastily scribble a few symbols inside the salt circle, copying them from an image saved on my phone. A few mumbled words in Latin, a drop of my blood in a dish, a quick—

Think very carefully, my Angel.

The shadows in the room intensify. A gust of wind ruffles my hair and slams the door. A familiar deep rumbling noise comes from within the very foundations of my little summoning warehouse.

No, no, no. This can't be happening; he can't have found me already. Not fair. I've had zero time to play.

"Fuck you," I mumble *for the thousandth time*, chucking the dish with my blood inside the salt circle.

There's a blinding flash of light, and a crow appears out of nowhere, flapping noisily within the circle, round and round the perimeter, cawing and flapping, round and round, shrieking, wings thrashing like a storm...

Another flash.

And silence.

The crow has vanished. And standing there, smiling, is a very naked man.

"Jesus fuck, where are your clothes?!" I gasp, because apparently his enormous cock is demanding more of my attention than the fact I've summoned a Prince of Hell, or that the Devil appears to have already found me.

His laughter snaps my eyes back to his face.

Ugh. Why are they all so beautiful? I get it, it's hot in

Hell. But come on, can't these pricks put their abs away for one day? Give the ladies a chance to breathe!

And where are the black eyes? His are a rich brown, warm and inviting, honest and thoughtful, trusting...

"Oh, no, you don't!" I bark. "That's your plan? Woo me with your ridiculous body and honey eyes? I'm sure that works on others, but can we get straight down to business?"

He lifts his arms, palms up. An open gesture of trust and friendship, a deceitful display of his cooperation.

"Do you talk? Or can you only caw?"

"I'm just waiting for you to finish assessing me and convincing yourself of my intentions. Which is funny, really, since it was you who summoned me."

I can still feel the shadows reaching out from the corners. Taste his blood on my tongue. Hear *his* voice whispering through my thoughts. ***Be careful, be careful, be careful...***

'You realize I'm out here finding ways to kill you?' I think to myself.

You're my Angel. No one gets to hurt you except me.

I already feel like an idiot before I say the words, but I go ahead and blurt them out. "The night is new and the raven has landed."

Malphas raises one curious eyebrow, looking me up and down with new interest. I blow out a breath of relief that my words meant something and maybe Lyra wasn't just screwing with me.

"Who are you?" he asks.

"Angel."

He should laugh at that. They all do. But he simply nods, like he already knew.

"What is it you need from me, Angel?"

"A ward. Strong enough to hide me from Lucifer."

Leave me now, and I can't protect you. Leave me, and you'll pay a heavy price.

"For how long?" Malphas asks.

"How long can you manage?"

"Well, that depends on how much payment you're offering, doesn't it?"

"From what I've read about you, it doesn't matter how much I sacrifice, you'll still stab me in the back. So, let's skip all the trading bullshit, shall we? If you're working with Lyra, then you know it's in your own interest to do this for me. I'll be assisting your war."

His lips draw into a line.

"And there's the fact that I've summoned you into a blood-infused devil trap. Give me what I want without expecting anything in return, or I'll kill you now."

Chapter
TWENTY

I'm dizzy. Confused. Running on instinct and adrenaline.

I just jumped into a metaphorical bed with Malphas, a Prince of Hell—who, by the way, took a little persuading to agree to my terms—and now, only hours later, I'm jumping into bed with a real-life angel.

We're on the same team.

I kill demons. He kills demons.

He shouldn't be glaring at me like shit on his shoe. But I suppose he's all good and holy and pure.

And I can feel my festering rotten soul seeping through my pores along with the sweat. I wipe my brow, my hand coming away with not only sweat, but Malphas's blood. I have to fight the twisted urge to lick it and compare the taste to a certain someone. I should probably have showered and changed before this meeting, but, you know, *ticktock*.

I think Remiel might be even more intimidating than the demon princes. I've never met an angel before. I'd rather avoid their sanctimonious asses. But Brooke pulled through for me, and here I stand.

I have to squint my eyes to look at him, to try and make out his features beyond the glare of light that seems to reflect into my face no matter what angle I look from.

He doesn't try to hide his wings. They vibrate gracefully behind him, buzzing with light and energy. So different from Lucifer's shadows...

Still, his power rivals the Devil's. It makes me squirm. I have this overwhelming feeling that I need to get on my knees and purge my sins. Like I need to apologize and start repenting. I press my lips together because I genuinely fear that I'm about to involuntarily spill my darkest secrets, like he's drawing them out of me—

"Remind me again why I would help you?" he asks, his voice light and delicate, not at all as imposing as the rest of him.

I swallow, making sure my guilty secrets are washed down and not about to tumble out when I open my mouth. "Do you want the Devil gone or not?"

He scoffs. "He will simply be replaced by another. It's the same cycle. Lucifer, Beelzebub, Satan, and the rest... they fight, they destroy, then claim power. Then they topple one another, and it goes round again."

"Well. Maybe I can take them all out, one at a time—"

His patronizing laugh cuts me off. "I can feel his evil inside you. You'll never be cleansed of it, even if you kill him."

"I'm not... that's not..."

"I work with hunters. I fight the war. I'll do whatever it takes to help maintain the balance. But I will not work with someone who doesn't have a genuine heart, and you, *Angel*, have nothing inside except lies. You lie to yourself, over and over, and you can never be free until you let the truth flow."

"Okay, you pretentious ass, I'm done with this." I get up into his face, despite the heat radiating from him, despite the way I feel like I might melt under his intense gaze. "Fine. You're right. The Devil fucked me, many times, and I *loved* it. And yes, I love blood and death and chaos. Happy now? Is that honest enough that you can work with me?"

His smile is so condescending that I reach for my blade, ready to cut it from his face. Angel or not...

He reaches forward, placing a palm against my forehead. Electricity jolts through me. I twitch like a bitch on hot coals.

Then he steps back, hands clasped, nodding.

"You will never be free of his sin, but I believe you will continue fighting for the right cause, whether or not it's what you feel on the inside."

"Are all angels so *preachy*?"

"Are all of Lucifer's toys so volatile?"

"Oh... Remiel." My head shakes. "Call me Lucifer's toy again, and I'll show you exactly how fucked up I am on the inside."

He simply nods again. Totally unfazed by the threat.

"If anything, it's Lucifer who is *my* toy!" I babble.

I can't see his face properly behind the light. It's infuriating. "And anyway, aren't we all just someone's toy? Who owns you, Remiel? I bet there's someone, and I'm not just talking God. Who is it that really pulls your strings?"

I catch the flicker across his face before the light becomes so blinding, I have to shield my eyes completely. My laughter slips out as I duck down instinctively, because the wind has picked up, but we're inside, and I can hear his wings flapping wildly. "Wow, that hit a nerve! It must be a woman?"

"Do not think you can affect me, mortal." His voice doesn't sound so light anymore. I try to peep through a crack in my fingers, but it's so bright my eyes stream. It feels like he's above me, though, hovering, his wings stirring up a storm. "You play with hellfire, and one day soon you might just burn. Choose your side wisely, because I will remember you, and if you make the wrong choice, then Lilith's armies will be the least of your worries. Vengeance is my favorite game."

"Lilith? Wait—"

Words spill from him, but I can't understand them. A constant stream that intensifies with every passing second. It could be Latin. Most likely Enochian.

My skin's on fire. Intense heat makes my throat burn, then there's a deafening clatter of metal on stone, and the angel is gone. I open my eyes, blinking to adjust to the now dim room, and find the most glorious blade I've ever seen lying at my feet.

Chapter
Twenty-One

"Angel? *Angel*!"

My eyes snap up to Brooke's concerned face.

"You've been staring at your drink for thirty minutes. What gives?" she asks.

What gives?

Oh, I dunno, I'm just running and hiding from the King of Hell, while simultaneously wanting him to appear so I can either kill him or fuck him.

Maybe both.

I've jumped on the crazy train and it's going too fast for me to get off. If I bail, I'm going to lose something along the way. My sanity? His touch? I either lose him or I lose myself. So, I'm clinging on tight, praying we stop at a station soon so I can just pause, take a breath, work this shit out...

"Angel?"

I shrug. "Malphas warded me from Lucifer, and it only took two hours of torture for him to agree to my terms, namely that he gains no sacrifice from me in return. And your angel dude gave me a blade after torturing me with his pious bullshit. It's going well."

"A little too well?" Brooke shakes her head. "Let me help you. For once, just take the help."

"You can't help me."

"Hey, I'm not that bad a hunter! I can handle—"

"That's not what I mean. It's not the killing part I need help with. It's the shit inside me. The storm brewing. The doubt and fear and pain."

Her eyebrows pinch.

"I think I... I think..." I can't do it. I can't say it out loud.

"What?"

"He's under my skin."

"Of course he is, honey! He's the Devil. That's his game. That's how he works. Once he's gone, you'll be all good."

"He's been under my skin my whole life. I just didn't know it. I'm not *right*, Brooke! I'm not like normal people or even normal hunters. I crave more. I seek darkness. I find comfort in things that should repulse."

She takes my hand over the table. "Look at me, sweet cheeks."

I study her soft brown eyes, the full lips, the kind face that hides just how good a killer she actually is. I wish I looked like her. I wish I could hide it. But I can't. I feel like my sickness is on show like a neon sign above my head.

Psycho here! Give me a knife and watch me go...

"Don't let Remiel get to you. He's not so bad once you know how to handle him, but you can't let that holier-than-thou crud affect you. He does it—"

"Brooke!" I gasp. "Are you... and him?"

"What? No!" she squeals, too loudly. "Anyway, what I'm sayin' is you're exactly the person you're meant to be. Okay, so you're a little rough around the edges, and maybe you got some kink going on, but I ain't ever met a more genuine sister. There's no bullshit with you. You are what you are. Own it! Like you always have. I don't recognize this self-doubt on you. It doesn't suit."

I shake my head, clicking my teeth quietly. "Brooke and an *angel*! How does that even work? I mean, is he allowed to, you know?"

"Shut your pie-hole!" She guffaws, slapping my hands on the table with a huge grin, almost as big as her tits, which wobble with her laughter.

Do I love this woman?!

For the first time, I realize I do. And that terrifies me more than anything else. I'm not supposed to form bonds. They can only end one way.

CHAPTER
TWENTY-TWO

I can't stop staring at the dagger.

Touching it.

Like some obsessed freak.

But it's just so pretty. So perfect. *Made for me*.

My trusty old Seraph blade forgotten, this Enochian one is next level. It *sings* to me in the sweetest lullaby! I hear it in my sleep. It taunts me both day and night.

It shimmers with faintly glowing symbols and looks as sharp as my tongue on a bad day.

But the blessed blade isn't the only thing haunting me. I can still hear Lucifer in my head. It seems he can still *connect* to me, but he can't find me thanks to Malphas's protection, and he's furious.

Is it so wrong that I find his anger such a turn-on?

Okay, yes, I know it is. But still... a raging Lucifer is HOT. There's nothing more mesmerizing than the sight of him losing his shit. The way his black eyes flare red. The way his muscles tighten. The way his wings coil behind him like shadowy beings. The way his skin starts to glow red when he's *really* losing it.

Then there's the *full*, scary all-out devil mode. Hulking giant of death and destruction. I probably shouldn't find that side of him sexy at all, and yet I do. Horns and all.

His whole pretty boy package is just a carefully erected disguise. A pleasant distraction from the evil inside with all that blond spiky hair, smooth defined muscle, and *lickable*...

I shake my head.

He can't hide his power, his darkness, no matter how stunning the form... and that's precisely what adds a whole extra layer of deliciousness.

Don't even get me started on the way he directs his rage into my sexual pleasure. The pain, the harmony, the way we fit together like magic. My body comes alive under his touch, ignited by his carnal desires.

The shadows don't intimidate me now. I want to fall into them and never come out.

My fingers slip inside my panties as I become lost to the feelings. I shiver as I imagine his breath against my ear, the way he whispers all the dirty and depraved things to me.

I rub furiously at myself, but I can't climax. I just can't quite get there. It's not enough. I need more. I need hi—

Then why are you hiding, my Angel?

My hand yanks back, eyes snapping wide-open like a

guilty puppy. I grab the dagger. But of course, he's not *really* here.

Don't stop. You didn't reach the finish line.

"I can't!" I whimper, sinking back onto the bed.

He chuckles through my mind.

"What have you done to me?" My voice cracks.

I brought you to life.

"I'm going to kill you."

Silence.

I shift uncomfortably, waiting for his response.

Still, silence.

"Are you afraid of me?" I yell.

Yes.

A sob escapes my throat. What am I doing out here?

I'm afraid of what you do to me, Angel. Afraid that you're out there and I can't protect you. Afraid that I could lose you. Afraid that if you die, I might explode so violently that the whole world will feel it.

"I'm not going to die, you drama queen." I sit up, fluffing the pillows.

You might. You don't know what you're messing with.

"Lyra and Malphas have nothing over me."

Lilith. Her name's Lilith, not Lyra.

And then it hits me like a ton of bricks. How did I not see this before? With a name like that!

"We're talking about *The* Lilith? Mother of demons?" I sit up straighter.

The one and only.

"What happens when you die and she takes over?" I cough, finding those words catching in my throat.

Much of the same. It's always the same shit in Hell and on Earth.

"No retort about how you're *not* going to die?" I feel the panic in my belly like ice.

You know, for someone so bent on killing me, you sure have some confusing emotions on the subject.

"Why do you even care about me? About what I do, or where I am? You must have accepted thousands of deals over the years. Why is claiming me so damned important to you?"

Don't play naive. You need only look inside yourself to know that answer.

"But *you* made me this way! That's cheating. You molded me!"

I did no such thing. Your father, though?

My eyes roll. Here comes more of the traitorous dad bullshit.

You've always thrived on death and destruction. There are only two scenarios when you truly feel at peace. That's when you have blood on your hands or on your tongue. And when you're under my touch.

Don't say it.

All those years your father thought he was training you to fight me, but all he was doing was making you more perfect* for *me.

"Oh, that's a good one!" I laugh, my stomach churning with bitter truth.

You do realize it's not me you're running from?

You're running from yourself. Too afraid to face up to what you really are. I told you my fears out loud, Angel. Now tell me yours.

"All right, enough pillow talk. I can't believe you're not strong enough to have busted through Malphas's ward yet. That disappoints me, Lucifer. Let's get this over with, shall we? Meet me tonight. I'm in Oregon. This ends."

I hate him. I hate him. I hate him.

I repeat the mantra to myself in case I bottle it. Lucifer is responsible for so much mess in my life. He's toyed with me, and he must pay.

There's nothing I'd love more than an angsty murderous reunion with you, Angel, but I'm a little tied up right now.

"Lyr—Lilith?" That bitch. I knew she'd beat me to it if I moped around too long.

She can't hold me for long.

"She has you *literally* chained up?"

Is that jealousy?

I snort. Too loud. Too quickly.

Don't worry, it's not in the kinky way. She saves that for human men.

There's a lump the size of a baseball in my throat. And I don't know if it's because Lilith is going to steal my kill, or if it's precisely that—she's stealing my kill, which means Lucifer dies.

I don't want my revenge taken from me.

And I don't want *him* taken from me.

"Arghhh!" I scream, clutching my head.

Do—

"Not another word! Just get the fuck out of my head, Lucifer."

His reply doesn't come.

In its place is his absence. The silence. The empty feeling in my core when he's not with me.

This can't happen. I don't know what I want the most right now when it comes to the Devil and his demise, but I do know that all options lead back to me, and I most certainly am not happy about Lilith being involved in any of it. I don't care if she's the damned mother of demons. She won't take this from me.

Sheathing my dagger, I pace the room as I think of a rescue plan.

I'm going to save the Devil.

Right before I kill him.

Probably.

CHAPTER
TWENTY-THREE

"I need a hellgate," I say, as Brooke leans over the table to scrutinize me. Her incredible tits create a canyon of a cleavage in front of me.

"Yassss, it's showtime? I just need to clean up a little mess from last night, then I'm with you—"

"Whoa there." I sit back, folding my arms. "You can't come, Brooke. You know I work alone."

"Na-uh." She kicks back, mirroring my pose. Stubborn bitches that we are. "Not this time. You don't get to take on something *this* epic without me."

"Brooke"—I sigh—"this is serious shit. I have no idea how to pull it off, but somehow I'm rescuing the Devil from *the* Lilith and her legion. It's not like—"

"Excuse the fuck me?!"

"Yes, I know you're a kickass hunter, but—"

"You're *rescuing* Lucifer? I thought you were on a mission to kill his repulsive ass!"

"Oh, right." My cheeks flare under her glare. "I am. I'm going to rescue him, then I'm going to kill him."

She rubs her face and pinches the bridge of her nose. "I've always tried real hard to understand you, girl, but you've lost me this time."

"It's complicated. I don't even understand myself."

Brooke's eyes widen in horror. "Oh, my sweet Lord! No, Angel, tell me no!"

I bite my lip.

"You're *fucking* the Devil?" she yells, and I about die, shrinking into my chair.

"Brooke! We're in a Haven. Keep your voice down!"

"Oh, right, because this news would be better suited to normal ears! Are you insane, bitch?"

"Yes! You know this."

Her eyes roll. She heaves out an exaggerated sigh. She leans forward again, pressing her fingers into her eyes. Takes another deep breath. Opens her eyes and offers me that ridiculously perfect pearly-white smile.

"I always wanted a trip to Hell. What should I wear? Is it hot as balls?"

I don't know what to say. I'm not sure I can say anything that's going to deter her, and dammit, I need her contacts to find a gate. That's the beauty of her running a Haven. She has an endless list of friends and contacts from all the hunters who pass through.

"All right, I'm going to clean up. Meet me back here at eight. I'll have my guy, and then it's road trip time, baby! Straight down the highway to Hell!"

I watch open-mouthed as she struts off, dark curly hair bobbing with the bounce in her hips. She's *excited*! That makes me even more nervous.

This is not going to go well.

CHAPTER
TWENTY-FOUR

"Remiel!" I shove Brooke's shoulder, glaring at the angel fuckwad behind her. "Your *guy* is Remiel, and you think I've got issues?"

"He's here purely to open the hellgate. He's not *my guy*."

I can't help snorting at her lies.

"Besides, getting involved with an angel is vastly different to getting involved with the Devil."

Remiel glowers at me. *Moody shit.*

"How does an angel have access to a hellgate, anyway?" I ask him directly.

"Do you want in or not? Because I don't have all night."

I raise my eyebrows at Brooke. "Seriously. Angels are miserable douchebags. You should try a guy with a little more humor, a little more—"

"Ohhhkay." She spins on her heels, shoving me forward. "Open her up, Remiel."

"With pleasure." He grins, drawing a sword that I swear wasn't anywhere to be seen before.

"Not *Angel*!" she shrieks, pushing me behind her. "The gate!"

Chuckling to himself, the sword vanishes. "Just demonstrating my humor."

Remiel pushes past us, mutters some gibberish, and a shimmering purple portal appears. We're in the middle of nowhere, some ancient forest that we had to hike through for an hour before she made a call and the angel materialized. I can't help glancing around nervously.

"Right then," Brooke says, steadying her breath. "Shall we?"

She offers me her hand, which I take, and we step forward. Remiel grabs my shoulder just before we reach the gate and leans into my ear. "Remember my warning, Whore of Lucifer. Choose your side wisely. Think of how he has played you your whole life and *finish* him."

I can't respond, because he shoves me and I tumble through the gate, still clutching Brooke's hand. We land on the other side, nestled between two rocky outcrops overlooking a demon... what? A compound? It looks like an army base. Buildings down one side and a legion of soldiers lined up in formation.

The words *Whore of Lucifer* still ring in my ears.

"I don't trust Remiel," I grunt.

"Me neither, but he does this thing with his tongue!" Brooke falls into me, giggling.

Yanking her out of sight behind the rocks, I can't help laughing too. It feels good. *Weird*. I don't laugh too much. Every time we try to stop, one of us catches the other's eye and we fall about again.

We totally lose it.

Is it the air in Hell? Is it the tension releasing? Is it friendship blossoming?

I have no idea, but eventually, Brooke comes to her senses and finally realizes exactly where she is.

"No way." She reaches out to stroke the stone, just as I once did, expecting the veins of lava to burn, but they don't. "I'm glad I went for the tank top." Brooke pulls it from her skin, trying to relieve the sticky, sweaty feeling.

"So, what's the plan?" she asks, peering around the rocks at the army below.

"Erm."

"Girl, tell me there's a plan?"

"Not exactly."

"Shit."

"I tried to warn you."

"Well. Remiel would have put us on this spot for a reason. We can assume it's Lilith's army down there, and that means Lucifer is probably holed up in one of those buildings."

"Okay, great, we just have to fight our way through the horde. You ready?" I stand, drawing my new Enochian blade. It hasn't yet tasted blood. I feel it vibrating with excitement.

"I'm thinking we should have brought friends."

I nod absently. If only I had some. The enormity of this task hits me, and I must admit my foolishness. If only I wasn't so damned anti-social and stubborn. "We need a distraction. We should have dragged Remiel through with us."

"Hey, I'm not done with his tongue yet! He can't die today." She turns to face me and her smile drops. "Angel, I don't know what messed-up shit is going on with you and the Devil, but are you sure about this?"

"No." I shake my head as she drags me into an embrace. It's awkward. I still have hold of my blade, and, hello... *cuddles*?!

"I'll never judge you for your choices, but a bitch might have to kick your ass if you don't finish this job. Lucifer dies, right?"

"Right." My twisted heart breaks.

Don't you dare come down here, Angel. I can handle this myself. Get the fuck out of Hell. Lucifer's raging voice erupts through my head, making me feel his power and his wrath all the way to my toes.

I laugh. "Too late now."

Brooke pulls back with a grim smile and a nod. "We've come this far."

Dammit, woman! I own you and you'll do as I say.

This time I laugh louder. "I'll grant you one thing—"

"What's that?" Brooke asks.

I frown. This communication thing isn't working out.

'Do I even need to talk out loud, or can you hear my thoughts?' I think.

I hear you.

I don't want to even think about what this means, about whether he's always been in on my thoughts...

Only because you're projecting them to me. And it's

stronger since you drank my blood. Occasionally, I've heard at other times when you didn't realize what you were doing.

Brooke shrugs at me, still waiting for my answer.

"I'll let you kill any demons you want but promise me that Lucifer is mine. And Lilith."

She nods in agreement. Lucifer growls in my head, making my toes curl. I love it when he's mad.

Poke the beast.

'I'm coming for you, demon. And as for owning me? Granted, you have owned me in the bedroom, but out here in the real world? Nope. Never happening. It all ends tonight.'

He's played me from birth.

I'm this fucked-up freak show of death and destruction because of him, because of the way my life was carved out.

My dad suffered all those years, waiting for him to come and take me. He damned well shot himself because of the pain.

Lucifer will pay.

✪

I MAY HAVE OVERESTIMATED MY ABILITIES. *AS USUAL.*

The demon legion below is massive. They seem to be carrying out some sort of drill. There's shouting, bellowing, darkness pooling around them. Even the eternally red sky has darkened over the compound. All of that demonic evil gathered in one place.

Lucifer is a constant rage inside my head. He won't

shut up. I might even call him frantic. *Desperate*! He switches from yelling furious orders at me to turn back, to offering quiet pleas, ones that I might believe were heartfelt, were they not coming from the King of Hell.

It's distracting having him pacing my skull while Brooke babbles nervously about how to get the hellgate back open so she can call for backup. We hadn't really thought that far ahead, about how to get back out of this shithole.

So now we're stuck, and onward is the only way to march.

Maybe we can sneak past them somehow? They seem pretty distracted by all the yelling. What are they doing? Why are they lined up? Surely too organized for the chaos of demons? Are they waiting for something? Maybe they—

"What in the ever-loving name is that?" Brooke spins on me.

It sounds like thunder.

'Shut up!' I inwardly scream at Lucifer because I can barely hear a damned thing over his ranting.

Get out. Now, Angel. Get away from here.

It's genuine panic in his voice, and that turns my blood to ice. Lead lines my feet as I try to step back.

The noise gets louder. A constant stormy rumble, deep and menacing. But the legion below us has fallen eerily quiet. They stand frozen. Poised. And the other noise becomes deafening. Angry, raging, thunderous...

On the horizon, a black mass appears.

Get. The. Fuck. Out.

'What is that?'

"What is that?" Brooke mirrors my thoughts.

That's my army. They're here to rescue me. See, you're not needed after all. Bye-bye, Angel. I'll come find you once it's over.

"It's Lucifer's army," I tell Brooke, marveling at the sight of this raging storm that approaches.

"Wow," she breathes, mouth hanging open.

I nod.

Angel! he yells. ***Last chance before this shit goes too far.***

There's a whooshing sound, and the hellgate materializes beside us. ***I just used up a shit-ton of my power on opening that from all the way down here. Don't say I've wasted that energy. Go.***

"Who did that?" Brooke asks, staring dubiously at the gate, drawing her weapon, ready for who might come through.

I shrug. "Go, Brooke. I won't be upset. Go back."

"And miss all this! Are you shitting me?" She squats down, back against the rock, settling in to watch the show. "We'll just sit here and let them wipe each other out, then we go down?"

"It'll be too late if we wait. Lilith could panic and kill Lucifer. Or someone could kill her. I want those deaths for myself."

"If Lilith had the power to kill him, she'd have done it already. Then again, how do we know she hasn't? What if we're here for nothing?"

"He's alive. I can feel him."

Her lips press together in disapproval. "I don't like the sound of that. Just how deep do you two go?"

The demon storm has reached the compound and the explosion nearly knocks me from my feet. With an almighty roar, the two sides clash. There's lightning, fire, vast plumes of black smoke, which could be from the fires, or it could be demon souls as they extinguish. Either way, the sight is horrific and glorious.

A war zone.

Blood and chaos.

My dagger sings and my soul stirs.

Casting aside Lucifer's concern, my feet carry me toward the action.

This is where I belong.

It's where I've always belonged.

On the battlefield. Blade in hand. The blood of my enemies coating my skin.

'All those years your father thought he was training you to fight me, but all he was doing was making you more perfect for me.' Lucifer's words echo around my skull, and I'm not sure if he's putting them there, or if it's just memories of the first time he muttered them. Either way, they feel so painfully true.

The opposing demon armies are so consumed with fighting each other, they barely cast a sideways glance at the two humans amongst them. Brooke and I are inconsequential. Not worth the effort when there's the real enemy to fight.

They ignore us as we slip between them, slashing and stabbing as we go. It doesn't matter which side we kill. If they're in our path, they die. Lucifer's army. Lilith's army. They're all demons and they all feel our blades.

We run, dodging the explosions of rock and lava, choking on the thick smoke that makes seeing farther than a few feet impossible. I have no idea where I'm headed, but it's safe to assume that Lucifer will be caged in the most heavily guarded area. So, every time the demons thin out, we adjust our path and head a different way, trying to find the real thick of the battle.

The noise is tremendous. This shrieking, growling drone—getting higher and higher in pitch like something's going to explode. Maybe it is.

I crash through the haze into the side of a building. "We've reached the buildings!" I declare triumphantly.

Brooke is heaving, not grinning like me. Surely, she enjoys killing demons. Otherwise why be a hunter?

"You enjoy this way *too* much," she mutters, leaning on the wall as she steadies her breath. Her hands are trembling.

"Are you okay?"

"Sure. I just need a moment."

"Not a good idea. You can't start digesting this shit until it's all over. It'll paralyze you and we don't have time for that."

She nods, just as two demons land against her,

crushing her into the wall as they lock hands around each other's throats. I grab one, yanking him away, slicing his guts.

The other pauses, eyeing me with delight. Honey-brown eyes. Friendly face.

Malphas.

I'm not sure what to do. And he hesitates, too.

We're on the same team, right? He helped me. He knows why I'm here.

But, at the end of the day, I'm a human. A hunter...

Oh, and there was the small amount of torture I put him through to force his agreement without terms. He seems to reach this realization at the same time as me, because we both swing simultaneously. He's faster.

His punch lands across my jaw. My skull rattles. Lucifer roars in rage.

I raise my arm, slashing my dagger toward his face, but he steps back and to the side, grabbing me into a headlock with one powerful arm.

"It's so good to see you again, Angel," Malphas growls, using his free arm to crush my wrist, forcing me to drop the dagger. He seems a lot bigger out here than when he was trapped in my warehouse.

Brooke tries to stand, but she's sagged against the wall, clutching her chest, and I think they might have broken her ribs when they crashed into her.

I squirm, reaching for the extra blade in my boot, but my fingertips can't quite get there.

Malphas snarls, grip tightening around my throat until I start seeing spots.

"Get off her!" Brooke launches at us.

Laughing, he releases me with a shove so hard that I travel ten feet and land on my back. Looking up, dazed, I see him grab my Enochian blade.

The world slows down.

I see it coming.

I can't stop it.

Staring right at me, he drives the blade through Brooke's heart.

"Noooooooooooo!" I scream until there's no air left.

I don't think there's any air left in the world. I try to drag it into my lungs, but it won't come.

"Looks like I got my sacrifice from you, after all." He grins.

My fingers finally find the knife in my boot as he stalks toward me. I fling it on pure instinct alone and it lodges in his neck.

He drops. His soul erupts in an angry plume.

I crawl to Brooke and collapse into her.

CHAPTER
TWENTY-FIVE

Get up, Angel.

I can't. I won't.

I can't let go of her body. Cradling her face. Willing her eyes to flicker back to life.

You need to move. Someone else will notice you soon.

Let them.

I don't care who notices.

Let me die with her.

The Enochian blade lies beside us. Coated in her blood. I can't touch it. Not now. I can't pick it up and kill Lucifer with it now. It's tainted with her death.

I caused her death.

I caused her death.

I sob into her hair.

No fucking people-ing! I knew better than to let her inside my heart.

I'm frozen in time. The war rages around me, but I don't see it. I don't feel it. I don't hear it.

My army is losing this battle.

"What?"

They're losing, Angel. You came here to rescue me, so get on your feet and rescue me.

I laugh.

It hurts. My lungs burn. My eyes stream.

Standing, I grab the blade. I no longer feel it singing. It's dead to me. I'm too numb. But I'll use it. I won't have had this weapon forged for nothing.

It killed Brooke, and now He will feel my vengeance.

There's an immediate tugging sensation in my mind, pulling me in one direction over another, and I know Lucifer must be getting desperate. I think he's guiding me. I stumble blindly through the battle. A few demons take a shot at me. I kill them in seconds. No thought. No emotion.

I'm nothing more than an empty machine of death. Rotten and broken. I don't deserve anything other than this dull pain. I'll let it fester. Soak up the rage. From now on, that's the only thing I'll feel.

Vengeance.

I made mistakes. I let feelings through. I broke my own rules and started to care.

Big mistake.

The pull in my mind stops, and I realize I'm here.

Dangling from a thick frame, up above the action, is a cage. No bigger than a closet. And inside those black metal bars, Lucifer sits.

His wings billow out behind him, through the bars and into the sky. Solid and yet *not*. They cast an enormous shadow over the battle below. His head presses into the bars. White knuckles clutching the metal. And his red eyes stare right through me, stripping me to the bone. I'm so raw. I'm just flesh and rotten insides.

I can't hold back the sob that leaves my lips. Furious and terrified and *agonizing*.

"What now?" I throw my hands in the air, staring at his pretty face and breaking on the inside to see him caged up. He's so full of raw power, I can't handle seeing him like that. I can't understand the look of sorrow on his face. Because I know it's not for himself, it's for me.

He has no right to look at me like that.

"Well?" I scream, slashing my blade into the nearest demons.

I don't know how I'm even standing because I'm sure I'm still not breathing.

I certainly don't want to. The overwhelming stench of exorcised demon is horrific. I've never experienced it this bad before.

He's still looking at me like he's in awe, and like he's sorry, and like he *loves* me.

Lilith is coming. He suddenly straightens.

I glare at him, still awaiting his plan.

See those symbols painted on the side of the building behind you? He points, and I spin to look. ***That's Lilith's hex. It's what's holding me in here. You need to break it.***

"Well, shit, I'm fresh out of explosives. Next plan?"

I feel his power building. The rise of his anger and fear. A faint red glow begins to form over his skin.

My shoulders slump. "Seems I'm not the only one to have overestimated my abilities here."

There's one way.

I already don't like the sound of this.

We're connected. Bonded. I can give you some of my power.

"What?"

Consider it a loan. It won't last long.

"Look, I know a few standard hunter spells. Breaking a hex created by Lilith is above my pay grade, with or without your power."

You'll never be the same again. My power won't stay, but a lingering essence of it will. You'll feel me inside you, more so than ever before.

"You're not selling this to me."

It's your choice. But you came here for me, and that's the only way I'm getting out of this cage now. Too many of my demons are lost. Lilith is nearly here, and she has help. She might just finish me—

That drags my ass back to reality.

Lilith is *not* taking this from me.

"Why bother? You know I'm going to kill you. I *have* to."

Ready?

"It's—"

A single thin plume of black smoke escapes his lips and rushes at me. In confusion, I try to swat it away like a fly, but it whooshes up my nose.

My body becomes a star, exploding in space, shattering into fragments before drawing back in on itself. I'm atoms rearranging themselves. I'm Earth and space and Hell and everything in between.

His dark power thrums through my veins. It washes through every part of my being, and I'm alive and dead, and nothing should feel this *incredible*...

The battle has slowed. Everyone's moving at a snail's pace. I see every action before it happens. I hear and feel and *know*—I just know every slice and slash before it occurs. It's so slow, it's all frozen.

Lucifer smiles.

Rage like nothing before blasts through my core, over my skin, into the air. Lifting my hands, every demon in my vicinity explodes into smoke and ash.

I can't control it. I need more.

Scanning the horizon, I reach out, feeling for whatever demons remain, *hunting them*—

The moment I sense them, they shatter beneath my power.

"Okay, enough playing. We don't have long. Break the hex," Lucifer speaks out loud for the first time in forever.

Break him. Kill him. End this.

Save him. Love him. Start again.

My mind whirs with confusion. My body ignites with power. My black soul screams for more.

I don't know where the words come from, but when I retreat to the building and press my palm to the hexed symbols, they spill from my lips in a steady stream.

"Move away," Lucifer yells.

I step back and the building crumbles.

I guess I brought explosives after all. I just didn't realize they were inside me.

It's only a loan. Don't get used to it.

His fingers brush along my neck. His arms wrap around me. He presses into me from behind. Too real. Too warm. Too soothing.

I look up at his empty cage.

Twisting into his embrace, I sob against his shoulder as his power ebbs from my veins.

"She's retreated," Lucifer finally says.

"Retreated? You fuck, she's *dead*!"

"Lilith, not Brooke." He eyes me like I'm a bomb and he doesn't know which wire to cut.

The Enochian blade pulses in my hand. He hasn't taken it from me, made me drop it. Does he really believe I won't do it?

"I hate you," I whisper.

"I know."

"You took everything from me. I could have had a life. A normal, happy life. Instead, my mother died, my dad went nuts, I endured an entire childhood of demons and death. And now I'm this sick fucking mess."

He nods.

"I hate you." My voice breaks. Tears spill.

"I also bring you peace. I give you what you need."

'All those years your father thought he was training you to fight me, but all he was doing was making you more perfect for me.'

"I *shouldn't* need that, though, should I? This shouldn't be my life."

"I'm your destiny, Angel. Don't ever say that we shouldn't be together, because there's nothing more right in the world than *us*."

"I can't live with the guilt. I can't be with you. It's not right. It's fucked-up and horrifically *wrong*."

"Maybe to a mortal mind." He shrugs, stepping back to force me to look into his eyes.

Or is he retreating because I'm gripping my blade tighter...?

His gaze travels to the weapon.

"That thing is starting to make me uncomfortable. Use it or lose it."

I glance down at the steel, symbols shimmering through the blood. It was forged for one thing. To kill Lucifer.

I made promises.

To Malphas.

To Remiel.

To *Brooke*.

Fuck them all, but not her. This blade has tasted something so horrific, something that should never have been.

Brooke.

My Brooke. The only friend I ever had.

Slowly, my eyes meet his. I step closer and stare into his wicked orbs for a long time. Sparkling black. Beautiful and ugly at the same time. There's the tiniest flicker of doubt on his face.

"I've tried everything for you, Angel. I've given you the punishments you crave, followed by the sweetest pleasures. I've dominated your body with ruthless savagery, then returned the favor, letting you take control of *my* body, straddle me, inflict your lust and hate however you pleased. I bled for you! Not only endured the attacks on my life, but I cut my throat and let you drink the blood of the King of Hell. I let you wake up in my bed. I attempted a date. I've offered you the goddamned throne at my side. What more do you want from me?" he growls.

"What do I want from you?" I reply, my voice a deep, low whisper. "You're the fucking Devil. I don't want *anything* from you."

I press the blade to his chest and drive it home, right to the hilt.

Time freezes.

Nothing happens for what feels like years. I suppose I expected his exorcism to be violent.

Lucifer is a storm. He crashed into my life after brewing on the horizon for all those years, finally unleashing himself upon me and obliterating everything I thought real. He's raw, carnal power. The darkest of energies. The mightiest of them all. Brutal, savage, intoxicating.

His ancient soul should have been purged with fanfare. It should have poured from his mortal body in an angry plume, blanketing Hell in perpetual darkness.

Instead, the glow in his eyes dims slowly. They seem to stare at me for hours, his face so pained, before his knees finally buckle and he falls. His mouth opens, and the darkness does pour out, right into the ground beneath our feet... but it's not rushed and vengeful. It's a slow, regretful retreat. Lingering, as if in the hope of some mistake, that it might not have to leave.

I drop to the ground. The warm rock bites into my knees as I pull his head into my lap.

It's done.

Everywhere is silence. Bodies are piled up as far as the eye can see.

Was his face always this stunning? I stroke his cheek. Silent tears *drip, drip, drip*... down my chin and against his skin. He's taken on an ethereal glow. Not red, not angry. It's soft and warm. More like an angel...

I'm a fallen angel.

I feel like I'm sitting in the eye of the storm, but I know his storm has already passed. This is the aftermath. Now is the time to dust off and rebuild.

But I'm not sure there's anything left inside me that can be repaired.

CHAPTER
TWENTY-SIX

FOUR WEEKS LATER...

I'M ACCUSTOMED TO LIFE ON THE MOVE. DAD NEVER STAYED IN one place too long. It's become part of me, this need to keep going.

'Don't mess around, Angel. You must be able to protect yourself. Kill and run. Never stay still.' He told me over and over again.

I turn the key in yet another motel door and dump my bag inside.

'If in doubt, run. Don't stay still. Don't let him trap you...'

"Too late, Dad," I mumble to myself. "He caught me. And now I'm running from an angel!"

I didn't need friends to hear the news. It spread like wildfire through the hunter community. It was impossible not to hear the whispers. Plus, it was all over our little secret internet hangout. I never get involved in hunter grids, but I like to lurk, keep an eye on the chatter.

An angel was on the rampage. He'd reportedly killed a bunch of demons in plain sight of humans, not caring who saw. *He's lost it*, hunters were saying. *Wasn't he the one that sometimes visited Brooke?* others would comment.

Hell hath no fury like a pissed off angel.

Remiel warned me.

I did what I promised. I killed Lucifer. But I also got Brooke killed with the very blade he made for me. I *knew* Malphas was the master of claiming sacrifice from those he helped. Arrogantly, I thought I had him. I should have known he'd get something from me in the end.

So, whether it's Remiel's own guilt pouring out or fury at me, I don't know. But I wasn't going to stick around to find out. Best to keep moving and hope to delay our inevitable encounter for as long as possible.

Then again, why bother? Maybe it would be better just to get it over with.

I no longer have his Enochian blade. I couldn't stand the sight of it. But it's not the sort of thing you can just dump, leave to fall into the wrong hands. In the end, after much deliberation, I took it to Brooke's Salty Haven. I told her friends and staff that she was dead.

Of course, I didn't give them the real details of what went down. I spun the story of us on a regular hunt that went bad. No one bought it. For one thing, they all know that the famous Angel works alone. And that she would never hand over an Enochian blade. Not to mention the fact that Remiel had probably been there looking for me already.

But there it was. I walked out the door and left them

to their grief and confusion. At least I'd managed to lug her body over the battlefield and back through the hellgate that Lucifer had reopened so she could have a burial. I don't know how I'd found the strength to carry a woman of her size that far. Maybe adrenaline. Maybe a lingering part of Lucifer's power...

Stabbing pain rips through my chest.

I grab a bottle of whiskey from my pack and take a gulp. And another. And another.

Until I'm suitably numb again.

CHAPTER
TWENTY-SEVEN

Days come and go.

Each one filled with more blood than the last.

I'm spiraling out of control. Slipping from my own mind. I don't know who I am or what I'm doing, or why I'm doing it. I'm just running on autopilot.

I've killed more demons in these last few weeks than ever before. Except, maybe, for the epic slaughter in Hell when I'd had Lucifer's power. Christ, I'd wiped out the whole of the battlefield, his own demons and Lilith's, and I hadn't even had to think about it. And that was just with a tiny bit of his essence. It's mind-boggling that Lilith managed to trap him at all.

I can still feel it. Some little part creeping around inside me. I hate it. I want it gone, but it lingers, reminding me constantly of what I've lost.

Because that's the problem here.

I've *lost*.

I'm alone. And I no longer have my dreams, my

comfort. There's nothing to soothe my soul. No one to tell me that it's okay to feel this much darkness, that it's okay to crave the destruction. *Because it's not okay.*

Dragging myself from self-pity, I prepare for tonight's hunt. It's ambitious. I've been following mysterious reports from a tiny little town in the wilds of Nevada. So remote that I can't understand how anyone lives here. But they do, all three hundred or so of the population, plus the gang of demons that are running the show.

It's a cult. Demon worshippers, sacrifices, the whole creepy shebang.

I've been hanging back for a week, watching, but it's hard to judge how many inhabitants are demons and how many are just demon-lovers. Regardless, they all pose a threat. I have to tread carefully.

They're naturally wary of outsiders. This isn't a place that you would just happen to pass through, but those I encounter seem to buy my story of being a geologist, here to study the weird rock formations nearby. I repeatedly tell them that I won't be sticking around long.

There's something going on tonight, though. The vibe in the town has changed. There's an air of excitement. People have been coming and going from the town square, setting up lights, speakers, and benches around a wooden stage.

My prediction—it's time for their monthly ritual. Probably involving sacrifices and a huge fuck-fest. And I have a suspicion they're planning on using *me* as one of the sacrifices. I've seen the way some of them keep sizing me up. Whispering behind my back.

A shadow snakes past the edge of my vision.

I keep seeing him. Feeling him.

And I know it's just my imagination, my desperation, but damn, it *hurts*.

All those birthdays that Lucifer would play with the shadows, taunting and teasing me, reveling in my unease. Now it's all I want—to have those shadows haunting me. I wish they'd linger for longer.

"Hey, lady!" A bearded man approaches as I pace the town square. "You done studying those rocks?"

I give him a blank stare.

"I found something out there the last week gone. Reckon you'll like it." He stops toe to toe, looming over me with his giant frame.

Sure. I bet you did. Don't tell me. It's in the back of your truck?

"It's in the truck." He smells like beer and piss and satanic ritual.

Yeah, that shit stinks.

I should know...

"Well, goodness me!" I beam. "You better show me!"

His shoulders relax. I follow him to the secluded parking lot behind the square.

Oh look. Here are all his buddies waiting by the truck to show me this find!

"Don't mind them," he mumbles, pushing me onward. "We got errands to run after we've given you this... rock."

Jeez. Do they really manage to capture women like this?!

The question now, do I kill them right here, blowing my cover and missing the chance for a big showdown tonight, or do I let them capture me and hope to fuck them over after?

The decision is taken from me, because evidently, I didn't give them enough credit. A hand sneaks from behind me, grabbing my face, and chloroforms my ass to oblivion.

I'M SWIMMING.

Like a bird, I fly through the ocean. My wings slice the water and I go on and on forever. Spinning, round and round, and upside down and over rocks and crashing and burning and drowning—

With a starved gasp, cold air invades my lungs and I shoot awake. Only, I can't move, because I'm tied to a cross, arms and legs spread.

Oh, thank the Lord! Lucifer has claimed me. I'm back in Hell where I belong...

Was it always this wet in Hell? Water drips from my hair, soaking through my dress. It's pouring rain. I'm so cold—

Dress?!

I glance down at my body. Lucifer did not clothe me in flimsy white *hippy* dresses.

"She's awake," someone says.

"Right on time," another speaks.

Well. Didn't this plan take a nosedive.

Drawing my head up, I look around at the hundreds of faces in the crowd. They gawk up at me on the stage. The air buzzes. They're all drenched too, but they don't seem to care. They're naked anyway.

So predictable. Sacrifice the sweet woman and then screw each other in a frenzy. Where's the originality? Do they really think Lucifer will get off on this shit?

Would. Not will.

Because he's not coming.

Which begs the question—who *will* come? This isn't a human cult hoping for a miracle. This is demon run. Despite the lack of originality, they must know what they're doing. So, who are they praying to? *Lilith?*

My skin erupts in goose bumps. I must kill her this time.

Three demon men have appeared on the stage with me. The crowd cheers until one of them, the leader —*Reynolds*, I know this from watching him all week— lifts a palm and silences them.

"This month, we have an extra special sacrifice," Reynolds says. "Hell is in chaos. It's time for a new leader to rise up. And with this offering, we will be gifted a place in the castle. This, my children, was Lucifer's toy *angel.*"

Well, fuck me. My geologist disguise wasn't so hot. Rumbles of excitement wash through the crowd.

"Shall we see if she glows on the inside like a real angel?" he asks.

The crowd cheers.

Fuck the endless angel jokes all the way to Hell.

I dig around in my core, trying to find the will to fight, but it's slipping away.

I've always belonged to the Devil. Let them sacrifice me to the darkness. Maybe my black soul will find his once more, somewhere in the abyss. Maybe I'll—

My thoughts shatter as a barrage of pain hits my stomach. Reynolds is punching me. In my stomach, my face, my stomach again. And then the dull pain erupts into something so much sharper. There's a knife in his hand and he slashes it over my abdomen. Not deep enough to gut me. But enough that I feel the blood seeping out, running into my dress.

I hear Lucifer's thunder and I know I must be dying. I've been seeing his shadows for days, but this is a new development in my psychosis. That distant rumble of fury that fills me with equal fear and excitement. It's so loud, my ears are bleeding…

Or is that my heart?

That's bleeding too—

Just *end* already! Why is death so slow? My eyes reach for the skies, and I pray.

Lightning flashes overhead.

And in that brief illumination, I see him.

He's like an apocalyptic vision of destruction.

The stars in the night sky vanish, robbed of their light by his darkness.

Nothing stirs. Nothing *breathes*.

Even the wind stops blowing and the rain stops falling.

He hovers above the stage, burning with hell fury before softly landing on the wooden planks. His wings settle behind him in vast shadows. Shadows that don't need the sun to form them because they're not of this Earth.

The entire congregation drops to its knees as one. Including the demon pricks on the stage. Shit, even *I'd* drop to my knees if I could. I know it's just a dream, my dying hallucinations, but still—

When Lucifer speaks, it's that growling beastly tone. "You have displeased me."

For a moment, I assume he's talking to me, because who else requires more attention right now than me? But he's staring down at Reynolds, who cowers before him. "She is mine."

"Yes, my King. But—"

"But?" Lucifer's shadow wings expand. The crowd collectively whimpers.

"We thought you were gone. We heard... anarchy in Hell... no one knew who was in charge..."

Lucifer's head shakes softly. Blowing a breath, he clicks his neck like this is all very tedious, and Reynolds explodes in a cloud of smoke.

The crowd finds their feet. They run. They scream.

It doesn't save them. Two more seconds pass and they're all incinerated. Humans and demons alike.

CHAPTER
TWENTY-EIGHT

Lucifer snaps his fingers and my shackles crumble. I fall, right into his embrace.

He's so firm. So *real*.

Did I die? Is it over? Is this Heaven, getting to feel him again?

There's no place in Heaven for me...

He scoops me up and carries me down the steps, off the stage, picking past bodies. I'm mesmerized by his face as I stare up at him, my arms looped around his neck. He looks exactly as I remember.

He stops.

Takes a deep breath.

And looks down into my eyes.

The connection knocks the air from me. I'm a sloppy mess of dead limbs and mangled thoughts.

A half smile creeps across his lips. "You're not dead."

"Yes, I am." I grin. I like being dead.

Leaning forward and lifting his arms, he brings my lips to his.

Soft. Tender.

Lasting an eternity.

"See," I mumble when the kiss breaks. "The Devil *does not* kiss like that. I'm dead, and I've reinvented you."

He chuckles, and the remnants of my heart explode. The deluge of tears breaks free.

He's real. He *is* here. I know it.

It's raining again. The stars are out. The world has switched back on.

"I've come to collect my angel, and this time I won't be letting go. No more games. Make your peace with *us*."

Draped in his arms, I submit. The relief is overwhelming. No more fighting.

"All those years my dad thought he was training me to fight you, but all he was doing was making me more perfect for you," I whisper.

I've been denying the fact that I belong to him. But I've been missing the bigger picture.

The Devil is *mine*.

Chapter
Twenty-Nine

Back in Hell, lounging in his bed, I have the unsettling and wonderful feeling that I'm *home*.

I've never had a home. We moved too much. Then, alone, I ran too much.

I glance warily at the hatch, which, once opened, fills Lucifer's chamber with the sounds of infernal torture. Then I think about all the other doors in the castle. What's behind them?

"See for yourself," he offers, joining me on the bed and pulling me into his chest.

Too normal. Too familiar. The Devil does not cuddle in bed.

I squirm awkwardly, but he just tightens his grip until I settle. My head rises and falls with his breath. But I can't hear a heartbeat.

"You're free, Angel. My castle is yours. Roam, kill, fuck... do as you please. Just make sure you return to me here each night, and that the *fucking* is reserved only for me."

I run my fingers over his abs. He feels like stone and magic. A mystical energy that seeps under my skin and connects us. Makes me want to hold him forever...

Who are we kidding? This is absurd.

"You know this can't ever work." My throat's dry with the horrible truth.

"Why?"

"Because you're... you, and I'm me! Seriously, a *hunter* and the Devil!"

"I love watching you work."

"You love watching me kill your own kind?"

"Demons are not of *my kind*. I've explained this before. I'm a fallen angel. They're beneath me. But yes, I crave all death and destruction, no matter who falls."

"I'll make enemies of other hunters. They'll want to kill me themselves if they find out."

"Since when do you care what others think?"

I consider that for a while, taking the opportunity to caress every part of his chest in case this never happens again. My fingertips tingle against his otherworldly presence.

"I'll never pledge myself in the way you want. I'll never kneel before your throne." I hold my breath, waiting for the fury, waiting to be thrown back into my cell.

"How about sitting on your own throne beside me?"

"What?" I shoot upward, staring down at his amused face as he continues to recline in bed.

"Angel, *Queen* of Sin. It sounds good, no?"

"You are, without any doubt, the craziest sonofabitch I've ever—"

"I release you. The deal your father made is no longer valid. I do not own your soul, Angel."

"Wh—" Something in my chest tightens. It explodes, implodes. This weight is sucked from my core. I feel it, the *shift*.

"You can walk away, and I won't follow." His smile fades.

"Seriously?"

"No!" he laughs. "That part's bullshit. I'd always follow you. But your soul is released. You're not chained to me."

Except, I am, aren't I?

And we both know it.

What the heart wants...

"I only ever wanted you to kneel for a moment, to pledge your loyalty, but I was always going to put you beside me. I did tell you that, numerous times. But I guess I can forgo the kneeling since you already do it so frequently for a taste of my co—"

"Fine!" I blurt, leaving the bed to pace the room, massaging trembling hands against my temples. I finally pause, facing him. "I'm yours, Lucifer. I'm done fighting it. You possess my heart and body. But I won't ever stop hunting. I'll never stop ridding Earth of your scourge."

His polished black eyes are relaxed. There's no angry red glow. He looks so comfortable, I can't work out what has given him so much peace. It makes no sense and it's not him and *none of this is right.*

He shrugs. "I told you. I love watching you work. It turns me on. Send as many of them back to Hell as you desire. They'll only keep coming."

"And I will keep fighting."

"Angel, as long as you warm my bed at night, take an occasional seat beside me, and scream for me in pleasure... then I don't care how many of my demons you slaughter."

My head spins. "What's with this U-turn?"

"I died. I had an out-of-body experience. My life flashed before my eyes. I saw the pearly white gates... *fuck*, I don't know, Angel! Maybe I just learned that I might have to make some sacrifices myself. I had time to think."

Memories of driving my blade into his chest batter me. The feeling floods back. That bottomless pit that opened in my stomach, the agony of losing him. I can't ever feel loss like that again. I won't. Don't I deserve some happiness after all the shit in my life? After all the lives I've saved, all the vermin I've taken out.

The Devil makes me happy.

"Why didn't you die? How did you come back?"

"I'm *invincible.*" His eyes almost roll. "I cannot be defeated."

"You knew that all along? That's why you didn't stop me from my deal with Malphas and Remiel? Or did you genuinely not know where I was?"

"I knew the second you left Hell. You were painfully

slow in getting Malphas to put his ward over you. I could have claimed you a hundred times over before you went off the radar."

"Why? Why would—"

"It was important to let you get it out of your system. You were never going to accept your true feelings until after you'd killed me."

I have no words.

"Though, admittedly, I started regretting my decision pretty quickly when I realized the danger you were putting yourself into with your alliances. It was reckless of me. I took a gamble, and it could have cost you your own life. Underestimating Lilith was another failing."

My head shakes.

"And what about after I killed you? It seems like convenient timing that you showed up right in my moment of peril. I could have sworn I'd seen shadows for days prior to that."

"Guilty." He shrugs. "I was waiting for the right moment."

"Watching me suffer?"

"Suffering is beautiful. It's so hard to look away from, especially yours."

"You motherfucker!" I launch at him, aiming a fist for his face, but he simply blocks and drags me back into bed. "You're a sadistic fuck."

"And you're mine."

"You'll never stop playing games with me," I groan.

"Wrong. I promise you, no more games. If you sit beside me, you are my equal."

"And lies drip from his tongue like falling rain," I say Jenna's words.

"Never to you. I didn't wait all these years to have you, only to treat you like all the rest."

"How would I ever know?"

"Because you feel me, in here." He presses a hand to my chest.

It feels too honest and raw and real. I *do* feel him inside. Lingering since the day he gave me his power. But was he always here with me, even before that?

"If an Enochian blade can't kill you, there's really nothing that can?" I don't know why I'm pushing the subject. Maybe a little future self-preservation planning for when this all falls apart around me.

"I don't think you can be trusted with that knowledge, my love." He chuckles, tracing paths up and down my back. Gentle fingers. Loving and affectionate.

Then he lets out a sigh. "I suppose an Enochian blade *could* do it, in theory. But you cried real tears for my loss. I can't ever be banished by someone who loves me."

His fingers pause. My heart stops. Then it jolts back at a thousand beats per minute.

"I don't... I..."

Fuck.

"Say it." His voice is a deep command.

And I can't stop my reply. "I love you, Lucifer."

CHAPTER
THIRTY

"I LOVE YOU, TOO," HE GROWLS, FLIPPING ME AROUND SO THAT I'm on my back and he's looming over me, hands beside my head, caging me in. "Since before you were even born."

He thrives off hate, not love.

"If I love you, won't you lose interest?" My voice is too high. "Surely, these last few months have all been about the fight. The chase. Trying to break me. If I submit, won't I become boring?"

He looks at me like I've lost my mind. "You've been paying no attention at all. *This* is everything I want. You are my destiny. You're the one to bombard me with *feelings*. Real emotions I've never felt before, and I won't be running from it, not ever."

The Devil doesn't have feelings.

His breath is against my neck. His lips graze the plane of my jaw.

He's a manipulator.

His teeth catch the lobe of my ear. His erection presses against his jeans between my thighs. His hips rock...

He's a liar. A fraud.

I grind upward, rubbing against him.

He's evil.

Forgoing the usual magic, he yanks my shirt over my head like a real man would. Rips the cup of my bra down. Captures a nipple in his mouth...

He can't possibly know love.

He worships my body like I'm an altar and his devotion is unparalleled. There are no whips. No chains. No blood. No pain. There's only his tongue and his hands and his *love*. His eyes are vulnerable, his face in awe. He's desperate and starved and giving me everything that shouldn't be possible.

I match him. He lets me touch him. Lets me taste and feel. Not in the way he did once before, when he bled and let me sample his skin, slick with his powerful essence. That was still wild and dark and devious. And I'll always want that. I'll always get off on the twisted ways we can hate-fuck each other, pushing the boundaries between pleasure and pain, bathing in sin.

But I can't deny how incredible this feels, too.

It's so slow and patient and I'm going to explode...

I love him.

"How is it possible for the Devil to take me to Heaven?" I groan as he licks between my legs, lapping me up like I'm honey.

"Heaven is overrated." He blows against my most sensitive spot. "I bring you to Hell and you love it."

My own groans drown out all further thought. I'm just emotion, sensation, nothing more. Drowning in his dark energy, gasping for breath, and screaming for more.

He gives. Then he takes. Then he gives, and round and round we go, a tangle of sweaty, trembling limbs. I kiss every inch of him. Taking the most time between his legs, sucking and licking and palming.

An eternity of exploring each other's bodies.

"You, my Queen, are the most beautiful woman in all of time," he murmurs against my nipple, fingers sliding between my thighs, teasing me to a whimpering wreck.

"And you, my King, are the most devastatingly delicious monster in all of time, but so help me, if you don't fuck me soon, I'm going to quit playing nice and start fighting you again."

Chuckling, he finally opens my legs and eases himself inside me.

No angry thrusts. No savage claiming.

Slowly, he withdraws. Gasps. And slides back in. I feel every moment, every sensation. I can't get enough. But it's too much.

Too much and I need more.

What is this madness?!

I love him.

We kiss as we make love.

I love him.

We cry out and we laugh and we *surrender*.

I love him.

And he loves me.

⬢

We don't leave the sanctuary of his room for days.

We spend every waking moment exploring each other. Taking our time. *Loving*.

He even has pancakes delivered to me on a tray.

Such a dangerous game of pretend we play. As if the Devil is really a man and not a selfish savage...

I groan as I take a bite, syrup dripping down my chin. "These are heavenly."

Lucifer leans across and licks the syrup from my skin. "I wish you'd stop talking about Heaven like it's the best of things on offer."

I nibble my lower lip. I put the fork back on the plate and push the pancakes away. There's something that keeps coming back to haunt me.

Guilt.

No amount of loving devotion from my Devil can erase *that* slicing pain.

"Brooke..." I whisper her name. "She's not here, in Hell, is she?"

"No."

Relief comes on an exhale of held breath.

"She's in purgatory," he says slowly.

"What?!"

"Hunters don't come to Hell, but they're a bit of a conundrum. They're doing God's work. It would be shitty of him and bad PR to allow them to be sent down.

But they *are* killers. They murder, they torture... they enjoy it." He eyes me appreciatively. "So, they can't go to Heaven either. Instead, they kind of slip through the cracks into purgatory. They're just waiting there, until me and His Holy Highness come up with a better plan for their transition. But currently, once they've suffered enough, he opens the pearly gates."

I can't breathe. "How long does that take?"

His lips press together. He looks at me like he's about to tell me my goldfish died. "A long time."

"My... my... Dad?"

My Dad is in purgatory?

He deserves it.

No, he doesn't.

Lucifer nods solemnly.

Like he actually gives a damn.

"I care about *you*. I'm sorry this is hard for you."

"So..." I wander across his room and pull on my cargo pants. No more parading around in lingerie. "How do I go about getting a meeting with God?"

He laughs.

I stare him down.

"You're going to be hard work, Angel. And I love it. But let's dip your toes into some Hell dealings first. Your throne awaits."

⬢

JUST AS PROMISED, WE SIT, SIDE BY SIDE, ON MATCHING thrones. My hand draped across in his lap.

"Lilith is regrouping," Lucifer muses. "She'll strike again, and we must be ready."

I nod in agreement. In fact, I can hardly wait for the opportunity to take her down.

In the meantime, one by one, various demons are brought before us with information, with *business*, or to be punished for some crime or another. Lucifer listens as I offer my opinions. He watches as I happily deliver the punishment to those who've earned it.

But there's something that keeps niggling me. Prickling down my spine in irritation.

And that's the masses of women gathered around the edges of the hall, engaged in a never-ending sex show.

"The concubines need to go." I turn to face my King. "The harem isn't—"

He snaps his fingers and every single one of them vanishes into thin air.

"What the fuck? If you—I didn't mean to get them all killed!"

"I sent them back to wherever they came from."

"You swear to me?" I feel like shit. "If you sent them anywhere nasty!"

He scoffs. "Some of the hovels I dragged them from were incredibly *nasty*, but you can't expect me to be on rehousing duty. They went home. Job done."

I blow a breath. "And where's Jenna?"

"Who?" Confusion on his face.

"The woman who tended me every single day in that cell!"

"Oh, you mean the traitor who aided your escape? She's somewhere in the inferno." He shrugs dismissively.

"She doesn't deserve that."

"She deserves the worst I can offer." A faint red glow forms in his eyes.

"You wanted me to escape!" I throw my hands up. "You know, to find my *true feelings*?"

"That's not the point. I can't let people betray me and get away with it."

"Please. She—"

"She's a serial killer. She hunted young men for five years before I took her."

"Shut the door! She always seemed so timid and compliant!" That woman was *not* a serial killer!

"Never underestimate my powers. I can tame even the wildest of souls. Bend them. Break them."

I give him a glare for the shitty way he's bragging about his depravity, the way he's smiling as he thinks about whatever he's done to her.

He clears his throat. "If I release her back to Earth, it'll go one of two ways. Either she'll be reformed and too terrified to carry out a single other sin, or she'll snap and be worse than ever before. More men will die."

"You're the King of Hell. Why do you care which way she falls? I thought you encourage that shit?"

"Obviously. But I still take my responsibilities here seriously. I'm here to punish those who sin."

"But you *encourage* sin! It's so hypocritical!"

"Fun, right?" He grins and I slap his chest. "Look, just

because she stuck her tongue in your pussy, you don't owe her anything."

"You arrogant shit! There's more to it than that, and you know it."

He sighs. I've got him. He's considering it.

"We'll keep an eye on her. If she *sins*, we'll bring her back," I offer. I can't help feeling like I still owe her, like I'm not done saving her. And I can't believe this serial killer nonsense.

He nods once. "But if she kills again, the next time she's brought back here it will be as a soul. I'll kill her and send her down."

I nod in reply.

Business dealings in Hell. My new life.

And so, it begins.

The Angel and the Devil, a twisted love story...

I only hope our happy ending doesn't ever fade. Because if it does, I have another blade lined up, and next time I won't cry.

EXCLUSIVE CONTENT!

Thanks so much for reading!

You can sign up to my mailing list to ensure you never miss new releases and for access to exclusive content, including deleted & bonus scenes, as they become available.

I also occasionally send out book recommendations, giveaways, and promos that I think you'll like.

SIGN UP AT
www.nicolarose-author.com

TWISTED GINNI

I'm known by many names — djinn, genie, demon.

I only ever get to call *them* one thing — Master.

Only this time, it's not one master, it's three.

Three beautifully haunted and damaged men, fleeing from the satanic cult that raised them. The apocalypse is coming, horsemen and all. If they don't stop it, their bodies will become nothing more than meat-suits to demon lords. Princes of Hell that are already seeping into their beings, battling for control.

Can I help them?

Well, that depends on how nicely they treat me. You see, I'm not a very *good* genie. I don't like following orders, I'm partial to twisting up my owner's emotions for kicks, and I'm running from my own apocalyptic fate — an eternity in purgatory for the crime of murdering a previous owner. *Oops.*

They're about to learn that summoning me brings a whole lot of fresh hell with it. If any of us survive this mess, it'll be a miracle.

Twisted Ginni is a full-length standalone Why-Choose / Reverse Harem romance.

BOOKS BY NICOLA ROSE

(Publication Order)

Broken by the Gladiator

Possessed by the Devil

The Elwood Legacy Trilogy

Her Dark Guardian

Twisted Ginni

Arrested

About the Author

Nicola Rose is from the UK, where she lives with her husband and two boys.

When she's not writing or reading, she can probably be found walking and cycling in the countryside, or playing boardgames in her pjs!

"Find me on social media, I'd love to connect with you!"

Nicola Rose's Romance Rebels
(Facebook Group)

TikTok

www.nicolarose-author.com
Nicola@nicolarose-author.com

Acknowledgments

As always, huge thanks to my family and friends for their unwavering support.

Thanks to my editor and team of beta readers — you challenge me, push me, and my stories are so much better for it.

I want to also thank the amazing, supportive author community. To all the authors and bloggers/reviewers who've become friends. For all the efforts to raise each other up.

Lastly, by no means least, thanks to you — my wonderful readers!

Printed in Great Britain
by Amazon